WHEN TO HOLD THEM

G.B. GORDON

A BLUEWATER BAY STORY

RIPTIDE
PUBLISHING

Riptide Publishing
PO Box 6652
Hillsborough, NJ 08844
www.riptidepublishing.com

When to Hold Them
Copyright © 2015 by G.B. Gordon

Cover art: L.C. Chase, lcchase.com/design.htm
Editor: KJ Charles
Layout: L.C. Chase, lcchase.com/design.htm

ISBN: 978-1-62649-295-0

First edition
August, 2015

Also available in ebook:
ISBN: 978-1-62649-294-3

WHEN TO HOLD THEM

G.B. GORDON

RIPTIDE
PUBLISHING

TABLE OF CONTENTS

D oran tried not to check the clock every few seconds. He had a website to finish and no time to go off daydreaming about a guy who didn't even know he existed.

He was quite familiar with the content management system by now, but by no means a coder, and it was always hard not to get distracted with Jace's phone chatter at the front counter, the ticking of the clock on the wall, the ads for bus tours and cruises playing on the TV screen above the waiting area. He struggled to tune it all out and concentrate on not screwing up the Bluewater Bay Tourist Information's website.

His fingers itched to check completely unrelated stuff, like his DeviantArt account, or how the Rainiers did last night, or if the weather was going to warm up anytime soon. Well, at least the weather was something he needed for his job, so it wasn't blocked on his computer.

Sometimes he was sure that the internet lock kicked him out of his groove worse than being able to check a piece of news, or his account, or the game. But then, of course, the lock wasn't about those pages as much as about TexasHoldEm.com, or FreePoker.net, and others like them.

"Hey, Callaghan," Jace called over after she'd hung up. "Wanna do lunch?"

Doran watched her log out and turn her desktop off. When she looked back up, he shook his head. "I'd rather finish this, before I lose my train of thought." He tapped his finger against his temple. "Squirrel brain. But thanks." Only half the truth. There was no way he was leaving now. For reasons. He couldn't wait for her to go. Not that she wasn't nice, but he wanted the next half hour to himself.

Jace shrugged into her jacket and wrapped her scarf around her neck. Which, since it was on the scale of a boa constrictor, took a while. "Don't starve yourself." She grabbed her car keys and purse. "Lock up behind me?"

He walked her to the door, exchanged the usual *Bye-see-yous*, and flipped the door sign to Closed. Outside, the sky hung low and gray over the roofs, a few flurries mixed in with the drizzle.

Only when Jace was out of sight did he dare a quick glance at the Gas'n'Sip across the road. Even though it was only noon.

The Tourist Information was still operating on winter hours, Saturdays and Sundays, ten to twelve only. Jace was handling the walk-ins and phone.

The director didn't let him talk to customers, much less handle any cash. Not that he blamed her. He was grateful for the whole reintegration program, and that she, or the council or whoever, had agreed to be part of it and given him this job. And she was nice about it. She covered her back, but she didn't make it awkward, and she hadn't told Jace about him. She'd even offered him free rides on the bus tours. Doran preferred to explore the town on foot and by himself. Still, he'd lucked out on this one.

But if he wanted to keep the job, he had to show them he was worth the effort. And he really needed for them to keep him beyond the probation period. He was not going back to jail. So he was putting the new accommodation guide together, both for the print brochure and the new website.

He retreated back behind his desk, but moved his chair over to the corner, from where he had a better view of the gas station across the road. Ten past noon. Almost time.

As if on cue, the white Silverado with the green stripe along its side and the National Park Service's arrowhead on the door pulled up in front of the pump. Doran watched the driver unfold himself from behind the wheel and, with a smile, tip his cap to ancient Mrs. Larson, who drove her behemoth of an antique to church and back at about five miles per hour every Sunday. Doran might be new, but everyone in Bluewater Bay knew Mrs. Larson.

Damn, that man's smile. It had burned itself into Doran's brain the first time he'd seen the ranger six weeks ago, just after New Year's.

His first week in town and on the job. He'd been idly watching the cars come and go at the pump when six feet something of relaxed confidence in a ranger uniform had gotten out of that truck, sending uncontrollable shivers up and down Doran's spine.

Doran had stared. He hadn't been able to help himself. The guy looked like Luther flipping West from *Resident Evil.* Or what West might have looked like if he wasn't fighting zombies.

After that, he'd seen the man drive up to the pump every Sunday, just after noon, and watching him had become an obsession. The long legs that made even those stupid green pants hot, and that looked still better in jeans; those fantastic shoulders. About the only complaint Doran had was that he didn't wear the Smokey-the-Bear hat with his uniform, but preferred a baseball cap or woolen hat with the NPS logo.

He was trying to screw up his courage enough to get a sandwich at the same time as the ranger paid for gas. Or a bag of M&M's. Anything, really. He'd been trying for weeks. *C'mon, Callaghan, you can do this.*

He checked his cash: five bucks and change. Not exactly plump. He'd get his pocket money for the week tomorrow night, but he'd still need to eat and buy the bus fare today. Shouldn't have bought those stupid lottery tickets. And a sandwich at the gas station wasn't exactly cheap. Ah, hell, if any gamble was ever worth the risk, this was it. He grabbed his keys and let himself out, then, in his hurry to cross the road, almost ran in front of a car. *Bonehead.*

The ranger stood chatting with the guy behind the register when Doran strolled in and pretended to agonize over his sandwich choice. He threw a quick glance over. The name tag on the ranger's uniform read *Xavier Wagner.* His gaze strayed higher and met an open, friendly smile, and warm brown eyes, crinkling at the corners in a way that made Doran's knees turn to Jell-O. *Oh god!*

Doran looked down because, gah, awkward. He tried to disappear into his hoodie, blindly grabbed one of the little plastic boxes from the cooler display, and went over to the cash register.

In front of him Wagner dug his wallet out of his back pocket. And, shit, that ass was just as amazing as the rest of him. When he flipped his wallet open, Doran immediately zeroed in on the gift card.

It was for Manscape Spa in Victoria, across the border. How could he possibly not notice something like that?

Which didn't necessarily mean anything. It was a gift card. He might never use it. And even if he did, there was still a chance he was straight. But. Odds. They were short enough to send Doran's mind into overdrive.

Long fingers slipped a credit card across the counter. Even that simple gesture was so together that Doran just wanted to shoot himself in the head and be done with it. Or sit in his lap. *Stop it! Poker face, Callaghan.* No, wrong thought. Don't think about poker. Don't ever think about poker again.

He almost missed his turn, and quickly shoved his five across. Wagner and the guy behind the counter obviously knew each other, easily chatting about the weather and the game. But as much as Doran wanted to catch every word, the details got lost in the way Wagner's lips curved and how the muscles in his cheek moved.

Doran pocketed his change, grabbed his sandwich, and fled before he did something even stupider than just stare at the man like a dumbass. He was lucky he hadn't gotten clocked.

Of course as soon as he sat at his desk again, he wanted to be back in the gas station. Just to get that smile again that melted his knees. *Please, let him be gay. Please.* Oh, who was he even kidding? It didn't make a shred of difference whether he was or not. The man's good looks and easy assurance were so far out of Doran's league, it wasn't even funny.

He looked back at the table of room rates he was putting together. Waste of time, of course. His eyes were magnetically drawn to the window and the pump beyond. Every time he checked his screen, he was starting from scratch because he couldn't remember a thing.

Finally he gave up and just waited for Wagner to come out. That sweet ache of longing when he finally did. Sorting his card and receipt, sinking the wallet into his back pocket, checking for traffic. That unaware swagger as he walked around his truck, *sweet Jesus!*

Doran gripped the armrests of his chair hard, just to keep himself from jerking off in the middle of the office.

Tuesday evening, Doran ghosted down to the basement room of the New Apostolic Church. He was early as always. The bus from Bluewater Bay to Port Angeles only ran a few times per day, and he was between cars at the moment. So to speak. He'd have much preferred to miss the GA meeting altogether, but that wasn't an option. At least this way he had his choice of chairs and could pick one as far on the outside of the semicircle as possible.

He drew his hood up as the room filled, trying to shrink into his chair and discourage any small talk. Times like this he really missed his phone. A little timewaster like Candy Crush would come in so handy right now.

Gamblers Anonymous wasn't as bad as the Homosexuals Anonymous had been, back when he was a teenager, but it still sucked. He didn't see how it would help anyone with an addiction.

When he'd first shown up here, they'd sat him down in a chair and swarmed him like locusts with their Twenty Questions, only to state the obvious from his answers. "You're a compulsive gambler." No shit, Sherlock.

It had been intimidating and a bit creepy, but nothing compared to his horror when he'd opened the little yellow booklet they gave him. He'd taken one look at the twelve points and known then and there that he'd have to fake it. The very language struck chords he thought he'd cut long ago. He was to admit that he was powerless, that he couldn't change by himself. Not that that meant he wasn't guilty. Oh, no. Only that he needed to trust in a higher power, humbly asking God to remove his shortcomings and praying for knowledge of His will. It had been like a kick in the face that sent him back six years into the past, into another church, where, with that same language, they'd tried to cure him of the other big "G."

Meanwhile, the guy in the front started his introductory reading from the pamphlet. Roger? Richard? Doran hadn't bothered to memorize any of their names. He wanted no part of these people.

With only twelve members it was one of the smaller meetings, or so he'd been told. Except for one middle-aged woman who seemed as uneasy as he was, they all knew each other. A good chunk of them had been coming here for years, some for decades, which, in Doran's mind, didn't exactly speak to the success of the program. He swallowed a laugh. Maybe next time he felt the seduction of a deck of cards, he should just think about how much longer it would keep him in the meeting. That should do it.

It had gone downhill from the introduction day onward. The more he tried to pull back, the more he was overrun with phone numbers and offers of spiritual fellowship, because *what's best for the Group is best for you*. All in the name of spiritual healing, of course. They instructed him earnestly about the concepts of Group Conscience and Unity, always speaking in capitals. There were a lot of meaningful glances in his direction as they talked about disruptive members, and how a Trusted Servant would reevaluate him when he was ready.

All of it so crushingly familiar. The forced reliance, the shaming, the sly grinding down of self until there was nothing left . . . Been there, didn't drink the Kool-Aid then, not drinking it now.

Back then it had been mainly his mother pressuring him to go. She'd been horrified when she found out he was gay. Furious when he'd decided he was quitting church and their flipping reparative therapy. If his aunt and uncle hadn't offered him their couch when he'd gotten kicked into the street, he wouldn't even have finished high school.

Now, though, he didn't see a way out, only through. He quickly got up for his spiel. "My name is Doran. I'm a compulsive gambler. I've hurt my family and owe money to strangers." It was the same three sentences he said every week, just so they'd lay off. After that he could tune out for the rest of the meeting, as one after the other got up to say their bit. Every one of them talked about gambling in one form or another, and if he listened, he just got antsy. They made his hands itch.

Before he could leave, though, he had to make it through the group hug, as he called it. The holding of hands and prayer in a circle. Maybe some of them actually got a sense of healing and acceptance out of this whole charade. They were welcome to it. All it gave Doran was the need for a shower.

He couldn't get away fast enough, even though his bus wouldn't leave for another half hour. Better sit in the cold and rain at the bus stop, than in here, where he couldn't breathe, where his skin crawled.

It had stopped raining, though, and there were even a few stars visible in the sky. Like a promise of fresh beginnings after all the hokey, tawdry crap. He wished he was already out of the city and back in Bluewater Bay where he could breathe. *Astounding Thoughts of a Boy from Tacoma, film at eleven.* His amused huff made a small white cloud in the evening air. He'd be camping out in Olympic Park next.

Which, wrong thought. Park. Ranger. He didn't want to think about Wagner, felt too rank after the past hour in that basement. Tainted somehow. Not that he'd be able to stop the thoughts now. At least not that way. He'd need a shower first.

He could think of how nice the guy had been, though. Of that easy smile he'd had for a stranger who'd been gaping at him like a total pinhead. Doran leaned against the upright of the bus shelter and allowed himself a few minutes of cheesy dreaming. And then a few minutes more until the bus pulled up.

Saturday he dropped the cover files for the brochure off at the print shop, then went over to the post office to mail his sort-of-weekly letter to his aunt and uncle. He wasn't allowed a computer or a smartphone, so this was his way to stay in touch, to tell them not to worry, and that he was on track with his program. He owed them that. No, he owed them a lot more, but this was what he could do right now. And it was easier than answering a lot of well-meant questions on the phone.

Back outside he pulled the hood of his sweatshirt up against the drizzle and headed across the parking lot. Only to stop dead in his tracks.

White Silverado with a green stripe.

No, wouldn't be him. Would it? This flipping town was right next to a flipping national park. Must be a dozen of those around. Although, maybe not at the ass end of winter.

He walked toward the parked truck as if drawn by a magnet.

The hood ticked softly in the cool February air. Doran wiped the rain off the side window, and put his hands up against the glass to peer inside. Shades clipped to the visor, GPS and what looked like a portable two-way radio on the dash, a travel mug in one of the cup holders, and some granola bars in the holdall behind them. Neat.

No trash. Two books on the passenger seat: *100 Classic Hikes in Washington* and *The Collected Poems of Langston Hughes.* Whoever that was. Really? Poems? Must be someone else's truck after—

"Anything I can help you with?"

Jesus, shit. Doran whipped around.

Wagner.

Towering over him. Close. So close. How had he snuck up on him like that?

Doran's brain screamed, *Run, run, run,* but his body refused to move. His eyes were glued to the strip of light-gray shirt visible under the jacket. Even standing up straight, he'd barely reach to the ranger's nose. But far from standing straight, he could feel himself shrinking into his hoodie, and against the cool side of the truck, water seeping into the back of his shirt.

Finally his muscles got the message, and he ducked to one side.

Wham! Faster than a man that size should be able to move, a hand shot out and slammed against the pillar by his ear. Doran's heart tried to climb out through his throat. And not in fear.

"Let's try that again, shall we?" Wagner's voice was level, nonthreatening, but taking no shit either. Its quiet rumble sent little shivers up Doran's arms.

A hand brushed against the side of Doran's hood, and Wagner stooped a little to look at his face. Warm fingers tilted his chin up. "You're the kid from the gas station."

Doran blinked to refocus, and searched those dark-brown eyes for more clues. He remembered that? How? Probably because Doran had made an ass of himself. He wasn't that memorable, otherwise.

"Let's go grab a coffee." Wagner moved him aside by the shoulders just enough to be able to open the passenger door. The books were unceremoniously dumped on top of the granola bars. "Hop in."

Nonono. "I wasn't going to steal anything, I swear." *Shut up, Callaghan. Just shut up.*

The look Wagner gave him was unreadable, but he said slowly, "No, I don't think you were, actually."

"Are . . . are you arresting me?" *Shut. The flip. Up!*

An amused twinkle crept into the eyes. "No. I couldn't, even if I wanted to. Different kind of ranger. I'm asking."

"Huh?"

"Starting to get pretty wet out here. And I think you owe me an explanation, kiddo."

No way. There was no explanation. *I have no clue who you are, but I've developed this enormous crush on you* didn't really cut it, did it? He wasn't even half-done kicking that around in his brain when he realized he was sitting in the car, with the door closed. *Breathe in. Breathe out.*

Wagner climbed in on the other side, and the truck dipped a little when he hoisted himself up. A ray of sunlight briefly cut through the clouds and reflected off the wet pavement as they turned into the road.

This time of year, parking wasn't a problem anywhere. Wagner pulled up in front of the Stomping Grounds, Bluewater Bay's incongruously hip coffee shop. He grabbed his mug and got out without a word.

Was Doran supposed to follow him? Or wait in the car until Wagner got back? No, staying in the truck was a really bad idea. Better to face him in a more public place than that. Shouldn't have gotten into a stranger's truck in the first place.

Oh, who was he kidding? Short of murder, there wasn't a lot the ranger could do to him that Doran wouldn't want him to do. And, hello, he really needed to think of something else here.

He scrambled out of the truck and ducked into the coffee shop. The kid behind the counter—Doran couldn't decide if boy or girl— sported a punk purple hairdo and took Wagner's order seemingly unaffected by that smile. Go figure. The smell of coffee and toasted bread made Doran's stomach growl. He could do lunch. If it didn't get stuck in his throat.

He checked his meager supply of cash and decided on regular coffee and a wrap. He always put ten bucks into his payback envelope as soon as he got his money for the week, and he always ran short toward the weekend. Which, he supposed, was the point. The program paid his rent, but they didn't want him to have a lot of cash. Well, duh.

Doran threw a quick glance at Wagner as he flipped through the newspapers on a table. They didn't talk while they waited for their coffees.

Wagner set his *triple shot topped with steamed milk, thank you* down on a table in the corner, and Doran followed him, mainly because he didn't know what else to do.

Wagner rested his chin on his thumb, index along his cheekbone, and rubbed his middle finger across an upper lip curved like the wings of a seagull. The well-groomed five-day shadow there continued along his jaw and around his mouth that still held the ghost of a smile.

Doran looked away. He was so doomed. He should have just walked past the flipping truck.

Not that he didn't crave the company, well, at least in his dreams. In real life, it would've been nicer if he could stop babbling in his head. But even if he'd wanted no part of the man, in a town the size of Bluewater Bay, you couldn't evade anyone who was set on talking to you. Not in the long run, anyway. *Oh. God.*

CHAPTER TWO

When he'd seen the hooded figure in the parking lot, peering through the car windows, Xavier had thought the kid was checking whether the truck or anything in it was worth stealing. Stupid with a marked car, but kids often were. Then he'd recognized the guy from the gas station. He could still have been casing the truck, of course. He looked so ridiculously young, though. More like he needed help.

"I guess you know more about me than I know about you," Xavier said, indicating his uniform and name tag. It was hard to see the boy's face under the hood. When he didn't answer, Xavier tried again. "That was your cue to introduce yourself, kid." On second thought, inviting him for a coffee had probably been a bad idea.

"Stop calling me that. I'm twenty-two." He flipped the hood down to the back of his neck. To, what? Prove it? Okay, he was definitely older than Xavier had first thought. And pretty. Xavier could feel his eyebrows going up.

The boy rummaged in his backpack and slapped a driver's license on the table. "Doran," he added. "Callaghan. I work at the Tourist Information." He vaguely indicated the direction with fluttering fingers.

Xavier tried not to smile. He doubted it would've been taken well. "Nice to finally have a name." He took a sip from his coffee, studying the face sans hood. So earnest and fragile. Eyes the color of blue noble fir. Full, sensual lower lip caught between teeth. *Whoa, there. Slow down, Hoss. A second ago you thought he was a teenager.* Only he wasn't.

Which was utterly beside the point.

"So, Doran, what's the deal with you checking out my truck?"

"I wasn't. I mean, I was, but not— I just wanted to— What I mean is, it wasn't for the truck."

Xavier laughed. "Easy, kid. Sorry—Doran." He set his cup down and leaned across the table. "If it wasn't for the truck, what were you checking out?"

Huge, open eyes one minute, a desperately-trying-to-be-fierce scowl the next.

"Doran?"

"I— From where I work, I can see the gas station. Man, I wasn't even sure it was your truck. I swear, I just— Hell, I don't even know, if you're g—" He bit his lip.

If he was what? Gay? Was the kid coming on to him? And why would that be the first thing that came to his mind?

Doran took a big swallow of his coffee, and then sputtered half of it back into the cup and in his lap, likely because he'd scalded himself.

"Whoa. Easy, kiddo. Breathe." Xavier took the cup out of his hand and set it back on the table so it wouldn't end up in his lap as well.

The boy's face shut down so hard that he gave Xavier whiplash. Xavier threw up both hands in retreat and leaned back in his chair.

"I saw you. At the gas station," Doran said.

"Yes, I know. You were standing next to me at the counter."

A questioning look came into those smoke-blue eyes, then the kid—Doran—studied his hands. "Anyway. I work across the road. Huge shop window. Goes out to the street. So, I see you." He started fidgeting in his seat. "Every Sunday." He stalled, then restarted, "When I saw the truck, I just wanted to see if it was you."

Xavier rested his chin on his hand. He was starting to get an idea about what was going on here.

Doran looked away.

"And what inside the car would tell you it was mine?"

"I don't know, man." Doran threw up his hands, then stuck his chin out. "Look, it was stupid, I get that."

Nothing slight or fragile about that chin. That was all stubborn sass and cornered challenge.

Xavier knew that special blend of vulnerable dignity firsthand, though it had been a while. A severe case of puppy crush. The kindest thing to do with that was to gently nip it in the bud.

He finished his coffee and slowly wiped his mug with the napkin. "Fair enough," he said, getting up.

A tiny frown appeared between Doran's eyebrows. One that just begged to be smoothed—or kissed—away. Christ, where had that come from?

"Do you want a lift back to your car?" Xavier asked, just to say something. He breathed a sigh of relief when Doran shook his head.

"See you around, then." He left so fast that he still had the crumpled napkin in his hand when he reached for his car keys.

Holy shit. What had that been all about? He needed to get laid. That would stop him from crushing on kids so much younger than him. Well, five years, anyway. Seemed more like ten. Although Doran had taken great pains to assure him it wasn't. *Not the fucking point, Wagner.*

"I'm here, Ma," Xavier yelled through the house the next morning. They'd insisted he keep his key because, according to his father, *It doesn't stop being your home, boy, just because you move out.* But he'd often thought there'd be much less yelling going on if he simply rang the bell. Not that she'd be able to get the door, of course.

His mother appeared at the top of the stairs holding up her index finger: *One minute.* They'd developed a sort of sign language since her stroke almost two years ago. He sometimes wished she'd at least given it a try when the doctors had told her she had a good chance of getting some of her speech back with therapy. But she'd listened to the garbled syllables coming out of her mouth for a few days, gotten quieter and quieter, and finally decided she was done talking.

Xavier strolled through the kitchen and stuck his head in the half-open door leading to the garage. "Papa? Are you in here?"

His father, towhead liberally covered in wood dust from sanding, peeked around the corner of a shelf. "Xav! Come on down, boy." He wore his usual Henley and bib overalls. Still a big man at sixty, he'd taught Xavier all about patience and control in a world that only reached to their shoulders.

Xavier took the three steps down to the concrete floor. The garage had never been used to park a car, but had been his father's shop since the day they'd finished building it. Business had picked up considerably with the movie people coming into town, and the prices they were willing to pay for handmade furniture bordered on the fantastic. Especially when it was quality work like that of Karl Wagner, who took pride in double dovetail joints and perfect lacquer finishes.

He still used a lot of the same tools he'd left Germany with as a teen, though he didn't sell out of his garage anymore. These days The Cabinet was a small store on Main and Eighth, where Debbie fielded walk-ins from custom orders and made sure Karl charged proper prices for his work.

"Still working on that cherry vanity?"

"Debbie picked that up on Thursday. I'm putting the last coat on the sink cabinet, and started on a dining set. Look at that flitch of maple Ron brought over on Friday. Isn't it a beauty?"

Usually Karl would drive down to the sawmill himself to hunt for unfinished planks with that certain je ne sais quoi that spoke to him. But sometimes, when Ron thought he had something special, he'd run it over right away. It was like a game between them of who could find the most striking piece.

This one had beautiful markings. Xavier ran his thumb along the bark, smooth enough to leave on for a rustic edge. "It'll make a stunning tabletop."

Karl winked at him. "Are you sure you don't want to work with me?"

Xavier laughed. "You know I'm much happier outside. I might need to add a new bookcase soon, though. I have to measure some spaces, then I'll come over to see what you have for me." He smoothed his hand lightly across the still-rough top of the plank. "You should take an apprentice again."

"If you bring me someone willing to invest the three years in a proper apprenticeship, I might. Otherwise don't bother. I'm not compromising on some snotty little I-can-learn-this-in-one-summer shit."

"There's gotta be—" He interrupted himself when he heard the hum of the stairlift through the open door. "Sounds like Ma's ready.

Have a good week, Papa. And don't sell that table before I've seen it finished." A brief hug that left Xavier brushing the wood dust off his clothes, and he ducked through the kitchen to help his mother into the truck.

Xavier was one of the few people she suffered to carry her, but he knew she hated it, so he merely gave her a hand up and handed her the seat belt. Ignoring the way she struggled with the smallest everyday tasks was one of the hardest things he'd ever had to learn. And it didn't get any easier with practice, either.

When he'd pulled up in front of the church, he hurried out of his seat and around the truck to open her door because she'd never wait for him. He had the perpetual horror vision of her slipping and falling the one day he wasn't fast enough to be there to catch her.

When he handed her the cane, she laid her hand on his cheek and gave him the long look that was her silent *thank you* for driving her, as well as *Good-bye, no need to walk me in.* And also an apology. For her needing to be here, when he couldn't be. Not anymore.

He'd known he was gay since seventh grade, but it wasn't something he'd flaunted in the small-town streets. Not that there'd been anyone to flaunt it with. That had changed when he went to college, though. Suddenly there was a truckload of gorgeous and available guys around him, and he'd reveled in the new opportunities and freedom, not bothering to hide.

Neither Lower Columbia nor UW had been far enough away for word not to travel back here. No one had actually said anything to his face when he came back for a Sunday service, but their squirming and whispers were enough to make him bristle. Bluewater Bay might have changed with the arrival of Hollywood, but some of its natives hadn't gotten the memo.

Well, his faith needed neither the building nor the community. The solitude of the park was enough, and at least there he could breathe. So he played the chauffeur every Sunday, and stayed outside.

He caught her hand against his face and placed a quick kiss on her head. "I'll be here to pick you up after. Don't run away, okay?"

The quip earned him the lopsided smile that was reward and curse at the same time. Like trying to draw breath against the wind.

He let her go, and climbed back into the truck, assuring himself in the rearview mirror that she made it safely inside.

He'd planned to do the week's shopping at the Safeway in Port Angeles, but a new sign over the general store had him pulling over. It had been Williams's General Store for generations, but old Mrs. Williams had put the place up for sale after her son had refused to take over, and it had stood empty all winter. *Your Daley Bread*, the new sign read. Someone had taped a *Now Open* sign in the window, and *We will honor your old points cards.*

When he'd been a child, Williams's had meant trading cards after a visit to the dentist. And later, loose change in sweaty palms for *those* magazines, which, he'd soon realized, were the wrong gender and a waste of his money. Mrs. Williams would push them across the counter in a fold of packing paper with the same fixed-above-your-shoulder stare a soldier might employ when faced with an officer whose decision he didn't agree with. She'd grown smaller as Xavier grew up, but he could always tell by her stare when one of her customers bought a copy of *Hustler* or *Penthouse* or *Playboy*.

He braced himself for finding the place unrecognizable as he pushed the door open. It had indeed changed, but not that much. The new owners had kept the counter and the floor-to-ceiling shelves behind them with the old-fashioned moldings. All painted white now, which allowed the black and white floor tiles to shine, and made the store seem twice as big.

The ancient till was still there, as was the lidded glass jar with the lollipops. The faded postcards had made way for cards *hand-painted by local artists*. Some of the brands had changed, and the shelf to the right of the door, which had held assorted hardware, now sported locally made organic soaps, honeys, mustards, and whatnot.

A tiny brunette roughly his own age came in through the door behind the counter, gave the grandmother of all starts when she saw him, and ducked right back out.

"Jackson," he heard her call with a Deep South drawl, "there's a customer."

Xavier gritted his teeth and waited for Jackson, and for an explanation that wouldn't involve skin color.

The man was short, but extremely well put-together. Midthirties, black hair just touching the collar of his white dress shirt, sleeves rolled up to the elbows, and a pair of jeans that put the lie to the suspenders attached to them.

He held his hand out to Xavier. "Jack Daley. Sorry about that. Margaret's a shy one. We really need to put that bell back up above the door, but the paint wasn't dry yet. I hope you haven't been waiting long?"

Southern accent, but not as pronounced as the woman's, and a rueful smile in the hazel eyes that did a lot to smooth Xavier's hackles back down.

He slowly took the offered hand and shook it. "Just a few minutes. Gave me a chance to look around."

"Hope you like it. Still needs a few touches here and there. We just opened up this morning. I thought a Sunday might be less busy, give us a chance to 'ease in.'" He air-quoted the last two words. And, yep, that was definitely a wink.

Xavier laughed. The guy was a bit theatrical maybe, but nice enough. Xavier had taken the two for a couple at first glance, but his gaydar was pinging loud and clear now.

"So." Daley glanced at his name tag and braced himself on the edge of the counter with both hands. "What can I do for you, Mr. Wagner?"

"Xavier is fine, or I'll feel like I'm back in class." He fished his shopping list out of his wallet and handed it over.

"Xavier it is." Jack scanned the list. "We don't have the beer yet. Still waiting for the license. Want me to pack the rest up for you? Paper bag okay? White flour or whole wheat?"

"Huh. If whole wheat's an option, I'll try that. No bag. I have a box in the car. I'll get it."

Local, organic, and paper bags. Definitely an improvement. Though Xavier suspected it would put a dent in his wallet.

It turned out not to be quite as bad as he'd feared. The difference was no more than he would've paid for gas to Port Angeles and back. Worth having the general store in business again, anyway. And Jack Daley was quite a character. Xavier stayed and chatted for a bit, then went to pick up his mother at the church. He took her to her friend's house for their standing lunch date, and drove over to the gas station.

Someone brushed hard against him on his way out. But since Xavier was a hard man to budge, it was the stranger who took an involuntary step to the side. Not without a glare.

Roy looked up from his Sunday crossword when he walked in. "Hey, X. Pump number one?"

Xavier nodded and hooked a thumb over his shoulder, indicating the door. "Who's the asshole?"

"Some bigwig from the studio. He's fucking important, and everyone else is gum under his shoe. I'm sorely tempted to refuse his sorry white ass service the next time he waltzes in here. You need anything else?"

"I'll grab a couple of six packs. Did you know the general store's open again?" He checked the fridge and tried to decide whether the Heineken or Stella was the lesser evil. Hopefully Jack Daley would go local with his beers as well.

"I heard it got bought, but didn't know they were open." Roy rang his two packs of Stella Artois up with the gas. "They don't have beer, huh?"

"Not yet, anyway. When are you going to stop stocking this crap, Roy?"

Roy shrugged. "People buy what they know. Or they ask a lot of stupid questions. Ain't nobody got time for that."

Xavier grinned and nodded at the crossword puzzle on the counter. "You being so overworked and all."

"Shut up."

Another customer came in, and Xavier made room and stashed his receipt.

It reminded him of the kid—Doran—standing there staring at him. *I see you. Every Sunday.*

He looked up at the Tourist Information across the road, but the reflections in the window didn't let him see anything inside.

Oh, get a grip, Xavier. The boy obviously had a truckload of issues, even if he was legal. Who needed that?

Unfortunately a lonely lunch didn't help in the slightest to shut up his intransigent brain. For some reason that stupid kid pushed his buttons.

Xavier didn't have the foggiest idea where the guy's crush had come from. Most people crossed to the other side of the street when they encountered him in the dark. He should have gotten used to that by now, but it never failed to irk him. To some extent the uniform offset the threat people seemed to perceive in him, but the last thing he'd expected was a skinny white boy with a preppy haircut carrying a torch for him. A pretty white boy, with dreamy eyes and a stubborn chin.

Eat your lunch, Xavier. He grinned at himself and checked his watch. Still time. Ma wouldn't mind staying for a little chat if he was a few minutes late.

Well, if Doran had some hidden strength, all the better for him. Now, think of something else.

Xavier let the field glasses sink and rubbed his eyes. He'd found footprints of M137 around a killed mountain beaver last week, but had hoped to catch sight of the big fisher for a visual assessment. They were as elusive as their marten cousins, despite being twice the size.

That was the only reason he'd gotten up before dawn on a Monday morning, and headed out when the moon was still a pale disk against the lightening sky. It had nothing to do with waking up repeatedly, short of breath, and with the evanescent dream-taste of supple lips against his own.

He slowly stretched first one leg, then the other. Clouds had started to drift in a couple of hours ago; the sky had descended and now hung as a gray vapor among the trees. It wasn't raining, precisely. Something between a fine spray and a thick mist that left tiny beads of moisture everywhere it touched.

His rain slicker was big enough to cover his backpack and knees, which had kept the tree stump he was sitting on dry so far, but even though he was used to remaining still for long stretches of time, his ass was starting to cramp, and he gave himself another half hour before the first shivers would run through his body and tell him it was time to move.

He eased the thermos out of his pocket and poured the last of the coffee. Only warm now rather than hot, but it might buy him another ten minutes.

He was screwing the cup back onto the thermos when he caught movement out of the corner of his eye, and froze. Ever so slowly, he stashed the thermos and got his field glasses back out, training them at the foot of the tree where he thought he'd seen something. Yep, there, the dark fur stood out against a small patch of old snow in the shadows.

Definitely M137. He'd lost one of his ears in a fight against a coyote who'd tried to steal his dinner. The coyote had been taught the error of its ways. Don't mess with a fisher, especially not one as big as M137.

He looked healthy, winter fur thick and glossy. No injuries Xavier could see as he watched the fisher wander across the forest floor, sticking his nose under roots and leaf litter in his quest for a snack beyond the picked-over bones of the beaver.

Only when the animal was out of sight did Xavier stash his field glasses and add the sighting in his log. Then he carefully stood up. He could almost hear his joints creak, he'd been sitting for so long. He flipped the little notebook shut, dislodging the folded leaflet about the preseason meeting at the Wilderness Information Center that night. He had half a mind not to go, save himself the drive into Port Angeles. On the other hand, he liked the people, and he should probably make an effort to stay in touch with colleagues and volunteers, and not turn into a complete hermit. The temptation was too great.

Between his father teaching him the scruples and responsibilities of men their size, his mother insisting on his caution and control in a racist world, and that world being scared stiff of who he might fuck, he'd grown up feeling like a bull in a china shop. The only way not to destroy anything was not to move.

Unfortunately he wasn't graced with a temperament that suffered arbitrary restrictions gladly, so he'd gotten the hell out of the china shop. He liked it out here. Even in the cold.

He stretched both arms above his head to get the kinks out of his back, before picking his way down off the ridge and to the next camera station. He'd just patrol those today; it was a raw day, good incentive to keep walking. Plus, he had some tension to work out of his system.

Maybe he'd hit Seattle or Victoria for a night on the town next weekend. He didn't do it very often, no point in crowds and meaningless hookups, but it would take his mind off its stupid obsession with Doran Callaghan's lips. Or so he hoped.

He couldn't remember being quite so preoccupied with anyone he didn't even really know since his school days. Not since Mr. Thompson, the new English teacher, had walked into his seventh-grade classroom with his poetry eyes and slender, sophisticated hands. Next to him even the senior boys had seemed callow and obscene. Xavier had been too shy, and not quite stupid enough, to do anything about his major platonic crush, other than to write painfully romantic poems long since burned. He'd been more comfortable hanging out with the girls, so he hadn't gone to his graduation unkissed. But, things being what they were, it hadn't led to anything.

He'd made up lost ground in college, but none of it had ever been very involved or exclusive. A sort-of-steady, on-and-off thing at university hadn't survived what his boyfriend had called Xavier's my-way-or-the-highway attitude. Xavier hadn't been particularly crushed. He certainly wasn't going to contort himself to fit expectations. Then or now. Staying by himself was easiest. That way nobody's heart got broken.

Which was why he'd walked out of that coffee shop. But whatever it was that woke him up at night was neither platonic nor uninvolved, and he had no idea what to do about it. Especially since nothing had actually happened.

Despite the morning fog turning to rain, he kept moving until the light started to fade, and actually managed to work some of the fidgets out of his system. He couldn't wait to get out of his rain gear and hit the shower. He stank. He didn't mind roughing it. He could be out in the park for days doing whatever needed to be done without noticing a lack of soap or change of clothes. But the closer he got to his shower, the more he itched. And every couple of weeks or so he granted himself a spa day. There was a simple, clean joy about a steam bath and massage, and having your whole head shaved by a pro. Yeah, that was definitely a better idea than a visit to the Tourist Information.

CHAPTER THREE

D oran kicked an empty pop can along the sidewalk to the bus stop. It hadn't really been a bad day. He'd managed not to buy any lottery tickets last week, so, unlike most Mondays, he'd had enough money left over for lunch and dinner and the bus fare. But Mondays came before Tuesdays, and Tuesdays meant GA meetings. Which meant Mondays were always kind of shitty. Not as shitty as Tuesdays, but shitty enough.

The day-long drizzle turned more and more into a light rain. It wasn't even five and already dark. He gave the can one last kick, then jogged the rest of the way to the stop. The hoodie was crap in the rain. He could apply for a voucher for a coat, of course. But it meant filling out forms, and handing in the receipt. Mostly, though, it meant that he'd have to explain what had happened to his old coat. Which he'd lost in a bet. So explaining that wasn't really an option. Maybe, if he went another week without giving in to temptation, he'd have enough for one of those cheap plastic rain covers that went over your coat. Those couldn't be more than five or ten bucks, could they? Of course they looked stupid as hell. But he'd be dry. That was worth some stupid.

The lights of a car swept the bus shelter with their glare, then passed. But instead of continuing on its way, the car stopped, then backed up. Shit. Creepy.

Doran stepped out into the rain, so he wouldn't be trapped in the shelter if he needed to run. The car, a truck, stopped right in front of him, the single streetlight above not enough to illuminate the driver. Wait. Was that a dark line running the length of the light-colored truck? That was a totally different kind of *Shit*.

The passenger-side window rolled down at the same time as the interior light came on.

"I'm going into Port Angeles. Want a ride?" Wagner said.

Sitting next to Wagner in a nice, warm car rather than next to some stranger on a smelly bus? *Hell, yeah.* Plus, he wouldn't have to hoof it from the stop to the probation counselor's office. He was already reaching out to open the door when he realized, damn, he'd have to tell Wagner where to let him off. Right. Not going to happen.

He froze mid-reach, then quickly turned the movement into a *no thanks* wave. "I'm good." A mumble that sounded anything but.

"Are you sure?"

"Sure." At least that came out a bit more solid.

"Suit yourself." The window hummed back up, and the truck moved forward. Doran watched it make a right about a hundred yards up the road. Which was weird, because there was no road there. Just the lot of a used car dealership that was closed now. Maybe Wagner was picking someone else up? Who? *None of your business, Callaghan.*

He turned back in the direction the bus would be coming from and leaned against the inside of the shelter, hands in his pockets, the damp seeping through to his sweater and T-shirt where his shoulders touched the glass, the rain a steady patter on the roof now.

How was he supposed to get Wagner out of his head if he ran into the man at every corner? And, whoa, Sunday.

He'd watched the gas station, of course, as he always did. This time he'd even had a voice to go with his fantasy. A quiet rumble that made little pebbles under his skin. He'd just been able to see Wagner through the windows of both buildings, where he stood at the counter, paying for his gas and whatever else he'd picked up. Beer? And then the ranger had turned his head and looked straight at him. One heartbeat. Two.

It was like being caught with your dick in your hand and your heart in your throat. Even when Wagner had looked away again, it had been several more heartbeats before Doran had been able to move again. He shivered at the memory, laid his head back against the glass, and looked straight into Wagner's eyes.

What? He was hallucinating now, and he hadn't even smoked anything.

"Merely wanted to double-check you're really okay." Wagner studied him intently, and Doran was sure he'd read his face like a book. "If you don't want a ride, that's fine, of course. But you ... You sounded a bit off."

Well, duh. Wild ideas of denying where he was headed ran through Doran's head. He didn't want Wagner to be offended. Especially not since he'd apparently gone to the trouble of parking his car and walking back here to check on him. But since only one bus stopped here, and that bus ran between Bluewater Bay and Port Angeles, that would not help to make him sound any more sane.

"I'm really okay." He didn't want that to be it, though, because then Wagner would just nod and leave. But he couldn't blurt out his fantasies either, because then Wagner would leave even faster. "I really wasn't checking out your truck," he added, just to keep talking. And it was only half a lie. He'd wanted to see what kind of person Wagner was, whether there'd be any clues to that in the truck. And he'd found a tidy reader of poetry. Who'd'a thunk it.

"Yeah, I know." Wagner braced himself against the glass, his arm so close to Doran's cheek that the sleeve would brush his face if he turned his head. That intent look was back in Wagner's eyes, and Doran forgot to breathe. This wasn't real. He watched a few raindrops run down Wagner's face and reached out to brush them away with his fingertips.

Then, maybe because being cocooned in here with the rain falling all around them felt so much like one of his fantasies, he stood on his toes and kissed Wagner's lips. Warm under the slightly cool raindrops, soft at first, opening with a surprised inhale. Then firm, pressing back, stubble against Doran's chin, Wagner's elbow touching the glass by his ear, his hand on top of the hood. The other hand running down the front of the hoodie to rest on his hip.

Doran slid both hands into the open jacket and around that big body that was so much warmer than his own. He wanted to wrap himself up in it, wanted ... he didn't even know what exactly. All of it. Everything.

Those lips on his, tongue and teeth licking and nipping, sent shivers of goose bumps all the way to his toes. A warm hand against his face, in his hair, thumb brushing his temple. Tongue dipping, teeth drawing his lower lip in.

The kiss grew more insistent, somewhere between gentle and demanding. The hand cupped the back of his neck. The shelter, the rain, everything fell away, leaving only the hard muscles under his hands, the taste and warm smell of the man, the moan rising in his throat.

Doran's knees gave out. But a strong hand on his buttocks held him up and pulled him against a distinct hard-on.

A bright light swept across his closed eyelids, and suddenly all that was left brushing against his lips was cold air.

He felt Wagner draw a shuddering breath. "Your bus." Wagner cleared his throat. "Your bus is here. Unless you want to ride with me after all."

Doran's brain wasn't working at all. "No." He meant the interruption, but Wagner took a step back, just holding on to Doran's arm until his knees locked again.

Doran wanted to bite his tongue off, take it back, but somewhere in the chaos of his mind lurked a reason why he shouldn't.

He didn't know how he'd gotten on the bus, except that the hand in the small of his back pushing him up the steps might have had something to do with it. Good thing, anyway, that he already had the fare counted out in his pocket. And that the driver was too busy checking for traffic to spare him a glance.

He stumbled into the first empty seat, huddled into the corner, hands shoved into opposite sleeves, trying to make up for lost warmth. His lips were still raw with that kiss, his body tingling. He let his head sink against the window and his brain find its way back to reality in its own time.

The bus pulled into the stop in Joyce, and the lights coming on made Doran blink. He had no idea what had happened back there. He'd kissed a couple of guys in his life, one who'd even been good at it, but that? How could a kiss blow him away like that? Who was the man behind the uniform, behind the name tag, to make him feel that way? There'd been an edge of inexorability in his voice, the day at the coffee shop, when he'd said, *Let's try that again*, that still sent furtive shivers Doran didn't fully understand along his spine.

He'd always gone for the bossy types. Unfortunately most of them were assholes. But Xavier, beyond the obvious good looks, had been thoroughly decent, even when he still thought Doran was casing his car.

The kiss must have taken him completely by surprise. But after that he'd been absolutely in control, breaking it off when the bus came, still giving Doran a choice. Which . . . Had Doran really kissed him? And Wagner had simply kissed him back. No, nothing simple about it.

But he *had* kissed him back. No rejection. Nothing faked. Wagner had wanted him. And with that the whole episode suddenly seemed totally unreal. Someone like Wagner to lean against on a cold night? Who'd slip powerful arms around him and have his back? That was movie material, not life.

By the time the bus pulled into Port Angeles, the buzz of arousal had died down, and the back-and-forth arguments in his head had left him exhausted and feeling strangely vulnerable as he trudged up the steps to Elena's office.

Normally, all he could think about the day before his GA meeting was how unfair the system was that got him stuck there. Not for punishing him in general. He'd had that coming, and gotten off fairly easy. But getting stuck in Gamblers Anonymous? That blew.

Today, though, all he could think of was that kiss. It had shifted things, or given him a different view. He didn't really know. But he suddenly saw the weariness in Elena's eyes when she said hi and offered him a seat. Did he really give her that much grief? Maybe it had just been a long day for her too.

She combed one hand through her short gray hair and settled back in her chair. "How're you doing, Doran?"

"Okay. I'm doing okay. Had a pretty good week." No lottery tickets. He didn't say that, though. He couldn't very well tell her about those.

She gave him a surprised smile. "That's good."

Really? Normally he just said, "Fine." He didn't quite see why *okay* would make her happier, but he'd take it. He started to squirm when she just kept looking at him. Had that been a question?

Finally she asked, "Anything special that was good?"

How about a kiss that made him feel like he'd never been kissed before? "Naw, just . . . stuff."

"You haven't been gambling, have you?"

Shit. "No! What would be good about that?" At least this week he didn't have to lie about that part.

"Nothing, really. I just thought you might consider it good if you won something."

Would he? Damn good question, that. But for now he needed to get her off the topic. She of all people must not think he'd been gambling. She could send him back behind bars with one signature. And it wouldn't be the county jail this time, either. "No. I haven't. I've met someone. Maybe. I mean, I have. But I don't know . . . Look, is it okay not to talk about this?"

"Yes, of course. Is there anything else you'd like to talk about?"

Pulling my toenails out? "Not really."

"Your meetings are going all right?"

Standard question, standard answer. "Fine."

The pencil in her hand did a quick *tap, tap* on the blotter. "You are going, right?"

Why was she questioning him like that all of a sudden? And on a week in which he'd been really good, too? *Bitch.* He dug the slip out of his backpack and shoved it across her desk. "All dates signed."

She merely glanced at it. "I see."

"And don't worry, these guys would not do me any favors. Trust me."

"You don't like them?"

Yeah, like he was going to complain to her. "It's fine."

She tilted her head to one side. "Talk to me, Doran. I know I'm here to make sure you comply. But I'm also here to help if I can. If there's something wrong, you should tell me."

Tempting. He didn't see what she could do to get him out of the meeting, but maybe there really was something wrong with this particular one and she could recommend a different one. Though two in a town the size of Port Angeles was unlikely. And Seattle was out without a car.

"I don't know," he finally said. "It doesn't feel right. But what do I know? I'm not quitting, though." Better make sure she got that. It hadn't been too bad, that one week in the county jail before his aunt and uncle had managed to post bail, but it had been a rude wake-up call. He'd been damned lucky his sentence had been suspended—first offense, restitution, sincere remorse, and all that. He wouldn't survive prison. He just knew he wouldn't. Not for a whole year.

"What doesn't feel right?" she asked gently.

He struggled to put his unease into words that wouldn't sound too aggressive or dismissive. "It doesn't feel like they're trying to help people get back on their own two feet. More like they want everyone to stay and toe the line. Like they're trying to convert people, you know? Like a church." He didn't understand how a court could compel him into what was essentially a cult.

"Well, the groups have Christian roots. But most of them are trying to be more inclusive these days."

"Have you ever been to one of their meetings?"

"No. Sorry. Can't say that I have."

"Well, this one's a lot like the church my parents dragged me to when I was a kid." That sounded like he was a godless heathen. Which was probably not good, right? "I know a lot of people find that helpful and comforting," he tried again. "But if it's compulsory, shouldn't there be, I don't know. I mean, isn't there supposed to be, like, a separation of church and state?" And what about his religious freedom? Had he forfeited that with his sentence?

Again the *tap, tap* of the pencil. "The whole reintegration program is pretty new, so I don't know off the cuff what your alternatives are, but normally . . ." She flipped through the Rolodex on her desk that looked old enough to have been inherited through at least three generations. "Tell you what, I'll make a few phone calls, see what I can come up with. Go to your GA meeting tomorrow, but I'll try to have an alternative for you by next Monday. Does that sound like a plan?"

Sounded a hell of lot better than his outlook five minutes ago. "It does. Thanks."

She gave him his money for the week and had him sign the receipt, then he was back out on the street, breathing a sigh of relief. That had easily been the best appointment he'd had with her so far. Maybe she really did want to help him. He probably shouldn't get his hopes up, but despite tomorrow's GA meeting still to get through, he felt as if a weight had been lifted off his shoulders.

He sailed through the GA meeting and the day after on his double high of a promise and a kiss, but as the weekend, and with it Sunday, came closer he started to fidget. What if Wagner hadn't meant it? The kiss? And what if he had? Would he show up on Sunday as usual? Would he expect Doran to come over and say hi? And then what?

He suddenly wished with all his heart that the man was his friend. Although . . . He couldn't decide if Wagner worked him up or relaxed him. Both. Sort of.

The only thing that saved him from blowing his little cash on lottery tickets during his lunchtime on Friday was the fact that it was raining cats and dogs. He really, really needed that raincoat. And he was not going to break into his payback envelope. He wasn't. It was a pact he'd made with himself.

He found one of those thin raincoats that folded into its own pocket for under ten bucks. At least it was black, so it didn't look too dorky. And it kept him dry, which meant reasonably warm if he dressed in his usual layers underneath. Didn't help the fidgets, though.

Back at the office he'd just managed to get into the zone, resizing images for the newsletter, when a shadow darkened the front door. The sign clearly said they were closed. Doran was pretty hard to see at his back-office desk, and extremely tempted to ignore whoever was trying to get his attention. He removed his earbuds just in time to hear a knock. Illiterate and persistent?

He moved his head to look around the side of his screen, and caught a flash of dark-green uniform that made his heart jump into his throat. He sat, frozen, while a voice screamed inside his head to get off his ass and open the door before Wagner gave up and walked away. It wasn't until the ranger indeed turned to leave that he got his legs under him and ran to the door. He'd never realized before how fiddly the key was to get into the lock.

By the time he'd gotten the door open and rushed outside, Wagner was halfway back to his truck. Doran wanted to call to him, but stumbled over whether to use his first or his last name, or both, and in any case, his throat was too tight.

Wagner stepped between two parked cars to get to the driver's side, threw a look over his shoulder, and, seeing Doran, stopped dead. Then he slowly turned and started coming back.

Doran was breathing as hard as if he'd run a mile. He couldn't watch Wagner without remembering how his body had felt pressed against his own, and when Wagner stopped in front of him, close enough to touch, Doran was as tongue-tied as always with this man.

For what seemed like forever, Wagner just looked at him. Finally he said, very softly, "Hey."

The single syllable fell like a spark on Doran's skin and spread heat all the way into his fingertips and toes.

Wagner spun him around by the shoulders and marched him back inside, out of the rain, then closed the door and turned the key, setting off utter chaos in Doran's head that included thoughts of being shoved against a wall, and images of scattered clothing. *Stop it!*

"I seem to always be asking this," Wagner said, "but, are you okay?"

Doran nodded.

"Look." Wagner rubbed one hand across his neck, then shoved it in his pocket. "I'm not entirely sure what happened Monday night at that bus stop. So, if I've got the wrong idea here, feel free to send me packing. No hard feelings, I promise." When Doran didn't say anything, he continued. "But I liked it, and I thought you did too."

Liked it? Understatement of the century. "Yeah," Doran got out.

His effort was rewarded with a heart-stopping smile. And an even more heart-stopping proposition. "Have dinner with me tomorrow. My treat. No strings attached."

Wow, poetry and dinner? Classy. And Doran had faded jeans and an eight-dollar raincoat. "Er, pizza?"

If Wagner had expected a more ecstatic response, he didn't show it. A twinkle came into the dark eyes. "Pizza it is. Seven? Are you working? Or should I pick you up at home?"

Seven was late to be working on a Saturday, but not worth going home and coming back here. Plus, it wasn't like he had tons of other stuff to do. He might even finish up the newsletter. "I'll be here." With that smile burning itself into his mind, frying the few synapses it had overlooked on its first pass, he was lucky that he'd scrounged up enough brain cells to answer direct questions.

Wagner reached out to touch his face and ran his thumb over Doran's lower lip.

At which point Doran's brain just gave up. White flag. Vacancy. He closed his eyes, and leaned into the touch. The thumb followed the contour of his upper lip, and Doran didn't quite manage to swallow a moan. It startled him into opening his eyes again.

The smile was still gentle, but more intense, somehow. "Yeah, so will I," Wagner murmured. He turned to unlock the door and left without another word.

The touch of his thumb was still searing Doran's lips, the realization that he wouldn't be kissed today slowly sank in, leaving him equal parts wistful and furious. He got back to his desk, but didn't even try to work again. Instead he fished for a pencil, wishing it was a No. 302 sepia art pencil that could do some real justice to the man's warm skin tone, dug his notebook out, and started to draw that smile.

The next day he was jittery pretty much from the minute he woke up.

As long as the office was still open, it was relatively easy to concentrate on the business at hand. They had a few people asking about tours for the set of *Wolf's Landing*, and one couple calling about accommodations for Easter weekend. And even though Doran wasn't involved in the customer side of the business, there was a constant hum of activity, underlaid with soft music and the ads playing on the screen in the waiting area that kept his brain chatter at a minimum.

But after Jace had locked up behind herself it got louder. He ate a sandwich at his desk and, for a while, managed to get back to work. But he soon caught himself watching the clock.

He couldn't remember ever having been on a real, honest-to-god date. One that involved dinner and being picked up. It seemed old-fashioned, decent, and thoughtful, and it gave him the warm fuzzies and hives all at the same time. What did one talk about on a first date? Surely it couldn't be full disclosure? He shuddered. Wagner was way too straitlaced for full disclosure. There was no fibbing about him, nothing cheap, no lies. His truck wasn't new, but in top shape with all the stickers and inspections, the uniform neat, his whole attitude polite and composed. Doran would've been surprised if he got parking tickets. Hell, he was the flipping law. The man probably didn't even jaywalk.

So, half disclosure? The basics, maybe? With a few strategic gaps? Those must be allowed, right? And then what? He soon lost himself in daydreams of thumbs across lips, and heady kisses, and a certain ranger out of his uniform.

By the time Wagner knocked on the door, Doran's webpage layout still looked like chicken scratches, but he'd finished a new sketch on his pad.

He grabbed his hoodie-raincoat combo and his backpack. Arms half inside sleeves, keys between his teeth, he struggled with the lock and setting the alarm, and all but tumbled into Wagner's arms.

"Whoa, hey there," was his amused greeting. He was out of uniform all right. Jeans and a soft, tan sweater with a quarter zip neck that screamed *Touch me*. Dreamy. Doran knew he'd have to sit on his hands.

"Hey," he mumbled around his keys, then locked up and stashed them in his backpack.

It had been a relatively warm day. Doran vaguely remembered one of Jace's customers talking about March coming in like a lamb or something. In any case, there was a hint of spring in the air as they walked the few feet to Wagner's parked truck.

"Since it's so nice out," Wagner said, echoing his thoughts, "do you want to walk? It's not far."

"Sure," Doran managed over his brain throwing out ridiculous shit like holding hands.

Wagner got his jacket from the car and led the way down Main and toward Flat Earth. Doran tried to come up with something to say, but was too busy keeping his hands in his pockets. What was it about this man that made him want to touch and be touched all the time?

Wagner opened the door to let Doran go ahead, and feeling Wagner's hand on the small of his back almost made him fall flat on his face.

It was a small place and Saturday night, but Doran caught something about a reservation over the blood pounding in his ears. This guy was seriously old-school.

"Both the house wine and the draft are pretty decent here," Wagner said.

"Beer's good." It would give him a chance to stay reasonably sober. One thing he really didn't need more of was chaos in his brain.

Wagner ordered two beers and a vegetarian pizza with extra cheese. Doran went with a pizza burger.

"Do you work every weekend?" Wagner asked.

"Yeah, right now Saturday and Sunday are the only two days we're open. Only until noon, though. I can take time off during the week if I want." He shrugged, almost added that there wasn't much else to do. But he wasn't going to admit that he didn't have a life. Or that his life was on hold. Though the only thing he truly missed was his Wacom and DeviantArt access.

"I sometimes take the weekend. But often just Sunday. Checking up on the parents." Wagner grinned. "But then I do for a living what other people pay for during their vacation."

"I thought they only had park rangers here in the summer."

"Mostly that's true. I'm the only one working year round, and only because I'm less involved with tourists and more with wildlife conservation. I'm employed with the National Park Service, but a lot of the work I do is for the Fish and Wildlife Service. So they pay part of my salary."

"So what, you're a scientist?"

"Yup. Ecology and conservation."

Doran hadn't even known that was a thing. He was tempted to ask further, but didn't want to seem even stupider than he already had. Maybe he'd check online, if he could.

They stuck with small talk and sports until their food arrived. Wagner had played more football than baseball in school. No surprise there. He'd heard of the Tacoma Rainiers, though.

"I won a weekend at their Youth Camp once, when I was fourteen," Doran said. "Best thing ever. They told me my pitch was impressive. I dreamed of making their roster almost every night." He grinned and shook his head at the memory.

"What happened?"

Being kicked out of home on my ass, for starters. He shrugged. "Life."

Wagner didn't dig, and they strayed to movies when Doran quoted Michelangelo. Because pizza. Apparently the local theater had a Frightful Fridays night, where they showed cult classics like *Slither* and *Tremors*. Doran hadn't even known the town had a program theater.

Wagner was easy to talk to, but so well-read it was scary. Doran didn't know half the books he mentioned. But they shared a love for graphic novels, and while Wagner seemed to be more about the story, he was quite interested when Doran started to get into different styles and artists, the use of color to set the tone, what medium he liked . . . He knew he tended to get carried away when someone got him started on his art, but Wagner didn't interrupt him once, and his attention never wavered.

Doran was sketching something on a napkin to illustrate a point about movement across panels when he looked up to find Wagner watching, not his hands, but his face, chin in hand, a small smile on his lips, and an expression in his eyes that felt like an intimate caress. There was a wink of enjoyment, but he also seemed to *see* Doran through every layer, like no one ever had, and not reject him. As if Doran could be a part of something if he wanted to. His train of thought derailed into oblivion.

Wagner let his arm sink on the table, palm up, and without hesitation Doran laid his hand in his, feeling the fingers curl loosely around his own, the thumb moving gently across his knuckles, sending tendrils of need up his arm.

"I knew I'd enjoy this," Wagner said, his voice low. "I didn't know I'd enjoy it quite this much. Your company. Thank you for coming."

The look, the touch, the voice banked up the heat until Doran was sure he'd burst into flames. "I, err, me too. Thank you. I mean, for the invitation. And enjoying, of course." *Just shut up, Callaghan.*

Wagner smiled. "Shall I take you home?"

Home? No. Not yet. Doran didn't want the evening to be over, but he nodded, afraid another string of nonsense would come out if he opened his mouth. He watched Wagner get up to pay the check, and crumpled the napkin into a little ball between his hands, wondering for the millionth time why Wagner even bothered with him. He never managed to get two consecutive sentences out that had a subject, verb, and object, except when he was boring Wagner to tears with something that couldn't possibly interest him. Only it had. Naw, Wagner was just too polite. No gambler in the world had that kind of luck.

When they stepped outside, Wagner zipped his jacket up and Doran buried his hands in the pockets of his hoodie. It was colder now, if not nearly as bad as it had been.

"Why don't you wait inside while I get the truck," Wagner suggested, but Doran shook his head.

He could deal with the cold. He wanted to draw the evening out. It would take longer if they walked. "It's not too far where I live. Maybe fifteen minutes?"

"Fine by me. If you're sure you're not cold."

Again Doran shook his head.

"Lead the way, then."

By now Doran didn't give a shit about *ridiculous* anymore, he really wanted to take Wagner's hand, feel the warmth of his skin on his own. He hunched his shoulders against the thought and dug his fingers into the hoodie's pockets to keep them from betraying him.

And then Wagner reached out and put his arm around Doran's shoulders, pulling him into the warmth of his body. Surely the man read his thoughts.

They reached the street, then the building where Doran lived. He was tempted to keep going, pretend he lived somewhere farther away, unwilling to give up his spot in Wagner's arm. But he must already have slowed down or something, because Wagner said, "This is where you live?"

He removed his arm, and Doran blurted out, "I need you to kiss me again." *Oh, shit.*

"If I recall correctly, it was you who kissed me."

"No. Well, yeah, technically. At first. But then you kinda, sorta, took over. Right?"

He couldn't see Wagner's face, because he was standing with his back to a streetlight, but he felt Wagner's fingers under his chin, tilting it up. "Like this?"

Warm lips touched his, slowly, deliberately taking possession, and it was a good thing no answer seemed required, because Doran had already forgotten the question.

The hand slid into his hair, the kiss got messier, lighting up every nerve in his body, and Doran's jeans grew uncomfortably tight even before the ranger's other hand cupped his ass and pulled him closer.

Doran slid both hands under Wagner's jacket, trying to fit himself as tightly against his body as possible. Only when he encountered hot skin against his palms did he realize he'd slid his hands right under the man's sweater.

He felt Wagner inhale, then gently try to disentangle himself, but Doran couldn't let go. Instead he pressed his face into Wagner's shoulder, wishing he could shut reality out and stay here.

Wagner bent his head and said against Doran's ear, "We should probably take this inside."

When Doran didn't respond, he said, "Or not. But then I should really go."

That brought Doran down to earth again. "No. Please." He stepped back and shrugged out of his backpack to hunt for his keys, then fiddled with them at the door, almost dropping them. "Please don't go."

Wagner covered his hands with his own, took the keys from him, and unlocked the door, then gave them back. "After you."

CHAPTER FOUR

D oran led the way up the rickety stairs, giving Xavier the opportunity to appreciate the view. When he wasn't thinking too hard about how he appeared or what to do or say next, Doran moved with a supple fluidity that made Xavier want to see him move somewhere other than the stairs.

There weren't that many apartments for rent in Bluewater Bay. Most people owned their property. This one was obviously rented out furnished. Xavier couldn't imagine Doran having moved in with either the 1920s' china cabinet or the oversized armchair upholstered in chintz roses.

"I'll be right back. There's some Coke in the fridge." Doran threw his backpack on the dining table, where its contents spilled across the top and over the edge. Xavier managed to catch the keys Doran had thrown on top, but a notebook hit the floor like a small tent.

Xavier picked it up, smoothing out the pages, and was about to put it back when he suddenly recognized himself. Or rather an improved version of himself, with a stunning smile. He flipped through the pages. There were some comic panels that looked like Wolf's Landing fanart, studies of people on buses, striking ballpoint renderings of the waterfront, and pages and pages of Xavier, getting out of his car, walking, sitting, or just his face. All of them so flattering that Xavier felt his eyebrows crawl toward his hairline. Puppy crush indeed.

The sound of a toilet flushing came from behind the door Doran had disappeared through, then running water. Xavier closed the notebook and returned it to the backpack.

Maybe he should leave. He had no idea how Doran expected this to go. The guy was such an odd mix of bold and flustered. But then he didn't really know what he himself expected either. He'd been drawn to Doran's looks. Hadn't he? Well, maybe his vulnerability as well. But things had shifted over dinner when he'd discovered an inquiring, creative mind behind the fragile facade. Suddenly the smoke-blue eyes had come alive with a passion that was entirely captivating and more than just a little sexy. But they'd also revealed how very deep that brittle vulnerability went.

Doran came back with a concerned crease between his eyebrows that cleared when he saw Xavier standing there.

"You stayed," he said as if he hadn't expected that. He threw his hoodie and what looked like a sweatshirt onto a chair. His black T-shirt read *Let Your Darkside Out.*

"I got the impression I was supposed to."

"Yes!"

Despite that fervent answer, Doran stayed where he was, as if now that they were alone, he didn't know what to do with that.

"Well, if at any time you change your mind, just say the word and I'll disappear, okay?" Xavier said. He was trying to come up with a way to put him a bit more at ease, when Doran suddenly closed the distance between them.

"No," he said. "I won't." Then he reached up and kissed Xavier. Taking him by surprise. Again.

Xavier wrapped his arms around him, feeling the long back muscle and the edge of the shoulder blade beneath the thin T-shirt, a little better prepared this time for the way Doran just melted against his body, though that mix of shyness and temerity still took his breath away. A natural spontaneity Doran didn't seem to trust, but couldn't quite suppress either. As if he wanted to trust, badly, but didn't dare.

Something beyond just sex was going on here. Trying to clear his head, Xavier broke the kiss. Doran leaned his forehead against Xavier's shoulder and seemed perfectly fine with just being held.

There was a layer here between the physical attraction and the meeting of minds that Xavier couldn't put his finger on. But it was nevertheless very much there. So much so that Xavier held Doran at arm's length and asked, "Why am I here, Doran?"

Doran blinked. "Because you want to be?" He seemed to be coming from far away, and obviously had a hard time wrapping his head around the question.

"Yeah, wise guy." Xavier nipped at those sinful lips, briefly giving in to temptation. Licking over them, finding them soft and compliant. He was losing himself in another kiss and pulled back again. "But what do you want from me?"

Doran's breath ghosted across his jaw as he asked, "Isn't that obvious?"

Xavier slowly shook his head. "That's just it. I don't think it is that obvious. There's something— What?"

Doran's eyes had suddenly focused in a way that put Xavier instantly on the alert. As if, in tracking a fisher through the underbrush, he'd scared up a rabbit instead.

"Something you want to tell me, kid?"

"Way to destroy the mood." Doran's gaze dropped, and he bent his head away to the left, exposing the delicious curve of his jaw.

Xavier fought down the temptation to trace it with his lips, brushed a couple of blond strands behind Doran's ear instead. But rather than lean into his hand as he'd done before, Doran moved away. He would have stepped back if Xavier hadn't held his shoulder, and he resisted being pulled close again.

Xavier let him go, but Doran didn't move, didn't look at Xavier either. When Xavier didn't reply or say anything else, he took half a step closer again, still not looking up. *Interesting.*

Xavier reached out to thread his hand through the straight hair, like silk between his fingers. He ran a thumb across one cheekbone. "Talk to me, kiddo."

"I'm not a kid. I'm twenty-two."

"Don't change the subject."

That little crease between Doran's eyebrows appeared again, and this time Xavier did smooth it out with his index finger. Doran flicked his head to the side, but didn't move away, some silent, hidden fight going on behind his forehead.

"If you don't want me to leave, you will have to talk to me," Xavier said quietly.

Now Doran did look at him, chin out. "Are you blackmailing me?"

"No." Xavier shook his head. "I'm stating a fact." He deliberately put some steel in his voice. "I won't tolerate secrets."

Doran stared at him. Yep, definitely a war going on in those eyes.

A car drove by on the street below, sending soft vibrations through the floor and walls of the old building. Doran started to fidget. Time to put up or shut up.

Xavier nodded. "Very well, then." With that he turned toward the door.

For a heartbeat there was no sound behind him, then a very soft, "Please." Hardly more than an exhale.

Xavier stopped, but didn't turn back around.

"You'll leave if I tell you," Doran whispered.

"I'm leaving now." He made himself move, open the door, walk through it. He'd half expected Doran to break. Doran'd been serious about not wanting him to leave, of that he was sure. That must be some secret.

He almost stopped on the stairs to wait. It took an effort not to. But he'd told the truth when he said he wouldn't tolerate secrets. They were no base for what could very well have been the start of something more permanent. He'd been tempted and willing to at least try for that. More so than ever before. But not with lies or secrets. That was a rule he wasn't willing to bend. He shouldn't have kissed the guy in the first place. His gut had told him he was trouble. He should've listened and nipped it in the bud like he'd been resolved to.

Now that the sun was down, the temperature dropped quickly. Xavier turned the thick knit collar of his jacket up against the chill. He was hunting through his pockets for the woolen hat when the door behind him banged open. He'd half turned toward the sound when Doran spilled through and straight into Xavier's side.

Xavier caught him when the impact almost sent Doran to his knees. His eyes were huge and glittered in the lamplight. "I'm sorry." He sucked in air. "I'm so sorry." But he didn't offer anything after that, just those desperate eyes.

Jesus fucking Christ. "Don't try to jerk me around, kid," Xavier growled. Doran squirmed in his grip, and Xavier, realizing that in his anger he'd tightened the hold on Doran's arm, let him go.

"I'm not. I swear, I'm not. It's just . . . I'm trying to, to . . . When you're there I can't think, but then, when you, when I—"

"Stop!"

Doran shut up as if Xavier had thrown a switch.

"Pull yourself together. Breathe. Then tell me. Last chance."

Doran stood up straighter, closed his eyes, and took a deep, audible breath. When he opened his eyes again, they held a here-goes-nothing look. "I'm fighting a gambling addiction," he said. "I screwed up. I owe a lot of money. I'm trying to pay it back. It's a program. I was going to my counseling meeting when you offered me a ride. I didn't want you to know." It came out in one big rush, as if he was afraid to lose his nerve. Now he hung his head, clearly awaiting Xavier's judgment.

Only, Xavier didn't know what to say. This was both more and less serious than he had expected. Well, he hadn't really thought about what he expected in any detail. "Gambling as in . . .?"

Doran shrugged without looking up. "Online poker, mostly. Scratch'n'Win, lottery tickets, a couple of bets." He shoved both hands deep into the pockets of his pants, shivering. Even in the scant light of the streetlamp Xavier could see the goose bumps covering his bare arms.

"You're freezing."

Again Doran shrugged, as if it made no difference.

Xavier ran a finger up his arm, trying to decide his next move. The shiver became a tremor.

"Right. Let's get you back inside."

He had to turn Doran around and march him back up the stairs, because Doran only moved as long as Xavier touched him. Not trusting that Xavier wouldn't disappear after all.

Back in his apartment, Doran was still shivering. Xavier, on the brink of telling him to put his sweater back on, simply opened his jacket on impulse, and wrapped it around Doran, pulling him close against his body. He encountered neither hesitation nor resistance this time. Doran fitted himself under Xavier's chin, and for a while they just stood there.

Xavier had never met anyone like him. Someone who had no fear of revealing his vulnerability and attraction. Well, beyond that little gambling problem, anyway. Who gave himself into his hands like this, despite the very real physical power imbalance. Someone whose body followed Xavier's every move, like a dancer followed his partner's lead. His reactions to whatever Xavier did to him immediate and unfiltered.

He'd never felt so protective and turned on at the same time. Protective and, yes, possessive. A grown-ass man should be able to resist that kind of puppy adoration, but it was more than that. It touched something deep inside him, something he'd never even suspected to be there. It was intoxicating and dangerous, because it made him want to ignore some powerful taboos he'd obeyed without question all his life. The thought sent currents up his arms, cold and hot, forbidding and enticing.

He ran his hands up and down Doran's spine until the shivers subsided, then tilted his head up and tasted those lips again. Took his time, licking and nipping, reveling in their supple softness, Doran's exhale against his skin, the reverberation of Doran's moan echoing against the walls of his own stomach and all the way down to his balls.

He leaned back just enough to watch Doran's face. With his eyes closed, his lashes painted faint shadows atop his cheekbones. Chinese brushstrokes on porcelain. So easily broken.

Well, he'd had a lifetime of practice with how to keep a lid on his shit. Until he figured out which direction this was going in, he just had to take it slow. And careful.

He slipped both hands under Doran's T-shirt and rucked it up to his chest, which prompted Doran to raise his arms over his head to be undressed. *Double syllable damn.*

Xavier dropped the shirt and shrugged out of his jacket, then pulled Doran close again. He immediately tilted his head up for a kiss, offering those impossible-to-resist lips. Xavier cupped his ass with both hands, felt the increased pressure on his cock all the way to his toes. If Doran's moan was any indication, so did he.

"Please," Doran gasped against his lips. "Bed."

So much for slow. He let Doran go. "Lead the way."

The bed was a gigantic affair of dark wood, shaped like a double sleigh. But Xavier was beyond furniture appreciation. All he could think was that it would probably creak like the dickens.

Doran had stopped in the middle of the room, waiting for whatever. Or was he waiting for Xavier to tell him what to do?

"You're way overdressed."

The dreamiest of smiles appeared on Doran's face. He opened the button on his pants and pulled down the zipper, then bent to discard pants, briefs, and socks in a swift two-step motion. All his earlier fidgets had dissolved. He stood relaxed, hands loosely curled, head down.

He wasn't as thin as he'd seemed under that oversized hoodie he wore all the time. Wiry, muscled arms, chest still filling in, but nice abs and extremely nice legs. Xavier made a twirling motion with his finger, and Doran turned. A fine ass too.

Xavier had expected him to start fidgeting again under the close scrutiny, but he was perfectly calm and surprisingly unembarrassed, his straight cock fully hard.

Xavier's pants were getting uncomfortably tight. He'd never practiced the steps of the dance they were dancing, but he knew what he wanted just the same. He stripped off his sweater and, when he saw Doran's eyes following the movement, crooked his index in a come-on gesture.

Doran closed the distance between them and touched the button on Xavier's pants, but then looked up with a question in his eyes. Asking permission?

Xavier nodded for him to go ahead.

Doran opened button and zipper, then stripped Xavier's pants down by going to his knees. Again with that grace that was so unlike the nervousness he usually displayed. He removed each boot with the pant leg as Xavier lifted his feet, then held his position for a heartbeat. Two. Head at Xavier's knees, spine bent in a continuous curve with his ass. *Jesus Christ.*

Very lightly, Doran skimmed his hands up Xavier's thighs and across the outline of his cock, looking up as he did so, watching him. Then he hooked his fingers in the waistband of Xavier's briefs and carefully shimmied them down around his ankles, stripping them off along with the socks.

Xavier held out his hand and, when Doran took it, pulled him up.

The touching of their naked bodies was electric. He heard Doran's harsh intake of breath and tipped his head back to see his eyes. Dark with dilated pupils. Xavier kissed him lightly and skated his fingertips up Doran's arms, across his shoulder blades, down his back. His response was a soft wispy sound, almost a whimper, and Doran pressing hard into his body.

Xavier held him at arm's length by his shoulders. "Turn the bed down."

He stood behind Doran as he complied, running his hand across the concave dip the muscle made in Doran's ass cheek as he bent over to grab the duvet. Then Xavier curved his hands around the hip bone on each side, placed a thumb in each of the dimples right above Doran's buttocks, and massaged the spot.

Doran nearly collapsed across the bed, barely managed to catch himself on his elbows.

Xavier gathered him close, pressing the length of his cock against the cleft between Doran's buttocks. He skimmed the nails of one hand up across his back and watched the goose bumps appear on his arms.

Doran was breathing hard, head hanging, hands fisting the sheets.

Twisting around to sit on the mattress, Xavier pulled him along between his legs. He leaned against the headboard, legs stretched out in front of him. Doran's back was against his chest, his head against Xavier's shoulder, strands of hair tickling his chin.

Xavier wasn't thinking anything, just playing, following his instincts, doing what felt good, what he thought felt good for both of them. He ran his hands across Doran's stomach, his chest, noticed the tremor when the tip of a nail grazed a nipple, and did it again, played with it.

Doran started to squirm. "Please." It made for shifting pressure and some friction between his lower back and Xavier's cock.

"Shh . . . Stop squirming."

A low moan replaced the movement.

Xavier ran his other hand lightly across Doran's cock, spreading pre-cum over the tip with his thumb.

Doran bucked into his hand. "Oh god, yes, please."

Xavier lightly slapped his thigh. "I said don't move."

This time he got a definite whimper. He grinned, resisting the need to shift his legs. Doran might be on a hair trigger, but he was close enough himself to avoid any additional stimulation. He feathered his fingers across Doran's cock and balls, taking a deep breath at the shiver that ran through Doran's body. Every time he skimmed across the stomach muscles, they twitched in response. Stroking Doran's throat and face with the other hand, he placed a kiss into his hair. "Remember what I asked you?"

No response.

"Doran? What do you want?"

"I want . . ." He turned his head just enough to whisper against Xavier's throat. "I want to be yours."

Holy hell. Now they were both fighting for air.

Xavier closed his hand around Doran's cock and moved his thumb across the well-lubricated tip. With an inarticulate shout, Doran came, in a series of hard jolts that slowly subsided to the occasional quiver running through his body. Xavier clenched his teeth against his own need to give in. He didn't want to miss one second of this.

One hand in Doran's hair, the other slick against his stomach, he kept stroking him through his come-down, until his chest wasn't heaving anymore.

"Okay now?" he murmured into Doran's hair.

He felt the answering smile against the skin of his wrist. "More than okay. May I move?"

Hot damn. He drew a shuddering breath at the thrill that question sent through his body. It wasn't right, Doran asking for permission, but shit, it went straight to his balls. "You may."

Doran rolled to the side, and knelt between Xavier's legs. He stretched his hand out, then stilled and looked up. "May I?"

"Yes." It almost came out a groan. Xavier didn't have enough air for more than one syllable. The boy was killing him.

Doran closed his hand around the base of his cock, then leaned forward and licked the length of it.

Xavier jerked so hard, he banged his head against the headboard, but the pain got lost in the lightning shock that seared every nerve ending when Doran closed his lips over his cock and started sucking. The heat of his mouth, the pressure of his fingers, the view of him kneeling there, sucking and licking, matching the rhythm with his hand . . . No control in the world could resist that.

Arousal tensed every muscle in his body and pulled his balls up. He had just enough time to push Doran off, before he shot all over his chest and stomach.

He was vaguely aware of Doran wiping him dry, then curling up in the crook of his arm. He'd wanted to ask something earlier, though he couldn't remember what. But as his breathing normalized he remembered the question he needed an answer to.

"Why do you want to be mine?" He wasn't sure what exactly he was really asking. Just that he needed an answer.

"I just do." Doran sounded sleepy.

"I'm afraid that's not good enough." Maybe he needed to know that he wasn't misreading the signals.

Doran raised himself on one elbow. "I don't know what else to say." All the winter storminess from earlier that night had left his eyes. They were wide and trusting, almost clear blue, with darker flecks around the iris.

Don't trust me like that, Xavier thought, *you don't know what I want to do to you.* "Think about it, because I'm going to ask you again."

Weak daylight trickled through the frilly curtains, heralding another overcast day. Xavier had a brief moment of where-the-hell-am-I before the puzzle pieces fell into place. He had a faint memory of jumbled dreams and waking up quite a few times during the night, having to check where he was each time.

He turned slowly to find Doran still fast asleep on his back. Cheek resting on one hand, facing Xavier, his other arm curled up above his head. His stomach rose and fell with deep even breaths. A faint treasure trail started just below his navel and disappeared in the riot of blond curls framing a case of morning wood that made Xavier wonder what was going on behind his smooth forehead.

He hitched himself up on one elbow and cupped that stubborn chin in his hand, tracing his thumb across the cheekbone. A frown appeared between Doran's brows.

Xavier leaned over to kiss it. "What are you dreaming of, gorgeous?"

Doran smiled without opening his eyes. "You bossing me around."

Xavier stilled. "You like that?"

Now Doran did look at him, his eyes still clouded with sleep, the smile growing shy. "You mean you couldn't tell?"

Damn, but the boy kept pushing that button Xavier hadn't known he had.

He was about to answer when his gaze swept the alarm clock on the nightstand: 8:16. He'd slept quite a bit longer than he usually did. "I'd better get a move on. Does this place have a shower?"

Doran made a face. "It's pretending to." He vaguely waved in the direction of the bathroom. "Feel free to use whatever you need."

Xavier's brow shot up before he could stop himself, and Doran caught on immediately, his eyes widening. But then, with a fierce blush flaming up his cheeks, he stretched both arms over his head. "Like I said . . ."

Xavier swallowed hard and moved his ass out of bed. He'd need to scrub his brain with soap before he picked up his mother for her Sunday service.

Despite pink tiles in the bathroom, the shower seemed okay, but when he turned it on he knew what Doran had meant. The pitiful trickle was barely enough to get wet, and he had to contort to get the soap off. He finger-brushed his teeth, then went to get dressed while Doran took his shower.

No books, he noted, idly looking around while he waited. Nothing personal, really, now he came to think of it, except a pile of notebooks and sketchpads on a small desk under the window, along with a collection of pencils in an empty Hellmann's jar. He itched to peek in the cabinets, to fill in the gaps of who Doran was. He suddenly understood why Doran had been checking out his car. Shoving both hands in the pockets of his jeans, he shook his head at himself. Stoopin' to snoopin'? No way. He'd been raised better than that. He also had the feeling that he wouldn't find anything, that what he saw was all there was. How long had the guy lived here?

"You want some coffee?" Doran asked when he came back.

Xavier shook his head. "I've got to run. Just didn't want to disappear on you."

"I'll walk back with you. Your truck's parked in front of the office anyway."

"You still have over an hour before you start. Didn't you say ten?"

Doran nodded. "I can grab a sandwich, and there's coffee at the office."

"Better haul ass, then."

Doran grabbed his backpack and the ubiquitous hoodie, but he didn't turn quite fast enough to hide his grin. Damn, if he didn't have a dirtier mind than Xavier did.

They were walking past the 7-Eleven when Doran suddenly stopped and hitched his thumb over his shoulder at the storefront. "Just gonna check on something. Won't be a sec."

But his furtive side glance told Xavier that something was off. Ancient toys in the window, faded magazines, stickers on the pane advertising stamps, cigarettes, Powerball, Mega Millions.

Lottery tickets. "Hold on."

Doran fidgeted. "Get you something?"

Xavier fixed him with a stare that had Doran blushing to the roots of his hair.

"Don't even think about it," he growled, then wondered what he was doing. He'd just met Doran, spent one night with him. He had no right to make decisions for him.

Doran shot him a hard-to-read glance from under his lashes. "None of your business." But he'd stopped on the steps up. His eyes, his whole body waiting, downright intent. Was he playing a game of chicken? He reminded Xavier of nothing so much as a fox cub who'd made off with the family dinner, only to stop and look back to invite a chase. A childish game, and a dangerous one that could easily lose him any ground he might have won so far against his addiction.

"You're making it my business," he said.

"I wasn't going to—"

"Don't lie to me, Doran." He resented being manipulated, which made his answer come out harsher than he'd intended, but he couldn't just let Doran sabotage himself either. If Doran hadn't wanted to get caught, he could have come here after Xavier had left, or at least been more subtle about it. Instead he was throwing it in Xavier's face. No, he wasn't stupid; he'd wanted Xavier to know. And for what, if not to be stopped?

Doran was staring fixedly at his feet now. Hands in his pockets, shoulders hunched.

Xavier had to stop himself from wrapping him up in a hug. "Doran?"

"I'm sorry."

"Are you going to come back here when I'm gone?"

A vigorous headshake was his answer.

Xavier allowed himself one arm around Doran's shoulder for a quick hug. "Stupid kid."

"I'm—"

"Twenty-two, I know. Take some damned responsibility, then. No more lottery tickets." He wasn't sure whether that would actually help, but had no idea what else would.

"No more lottery tickets." The echo was a bit of a mumble, so Xavier held out his hand.

"Your word?"

Now Doran did look up at him. His eyebrows went from insecure slants to a knot of determination in a fascinating display of emotions. Xavier had never seen eyebrows that so demanded kissing.

Doran took his offered hand. "You have my word."

That afternoon, when Xavier brought his mother home from her lunch, he didn't leave after escorting her inside, but sauntered into the garage, where he answered his father's raised eyebrows with, "Thought I'd check if you have any boards lying around for that bookcase I mentioned."

He wasn't looking at his father, but knew from the minute of pregnant silence that he hadn't bought Xavier's casual attitude.

Karl didn't call him on his theatrics, though. "Let's check the shed. I should have something usable in there."

The shed was the size of a small barn with shelves of lumber on three sides, all the way up to the rafters. Xavier loved the smell of it, always had. If at five he'd wanted to be a lumberjack, it was because of the cut-wood smell in the shed.

"Are you alright, Xav?"

"Yeah." He wasn't too sure why he'd come home. On the one hand, his father had always been the one he'd come to with problems. There was no one else. On the other hand, there were things you simply didn't discuss with your parents. "I've met someone," he said to explain his reluctance, so his father wouldn't think he was dismissing him.

His father ran a hand over one of the boards and threw him a quick sideways look. "And it's complicated?"

"I don't know. Yeah. Maybe."

"I see. This reclaimed maple floor might be just the ticket. It's sturdy enough, and the paint needs sanding off." Deliberately chosen because it would keep his hands busy and his mind free to puzzle shit out.

"Thanks."

They moved the planks into the shop, and Xavier made himself a sanding block. Working by hand was what he needed now. He might even go to plain fingers and sandpaper later. He didn't want to even the surface out too much, at least for the upright pieces. The footworn dips gave the wood history and character that he didn't want to take away.

They worked in silence for a while, each in their own corner, busy with their own pieces.

"Papa, can you take off your dad hat for a second?"

"I don't know. Try me."

"Am I a nice guy?" Xavier didn't break his rhythm, but his shoulders tensed, waiting for the answer.

"'Nice' lacks definition. It could mean anything between decent and doormat. You're loving, respectful, honorable . . . certainly not a doormat. What are you asking me?"

"I'm not sure." Still, it had been what he'd needed to hear. "Maybe when I figure that out I won't need to ask anymore."

Didn't everyone want to be one of the good guys? He'd tried all his life to do the right thing, no matter what everyone else said. And while that wasn't always easy, he'd never had a serious doubt about what the right thing was. Now, though? "Honorable, huh?"

There was a brief pause, before his father asked, "Did you do something that makes you question that?"

"No." *Not yet.* "I'm questioning what I'm thinking. What I want to do."

"Then, maybe, don't do it."

Xavier breathed a resigned laugh. "Yeah, that's what I've been trying, but I'm questioning that too."

His father stopped working, turned and leaned against his workbench, wiping his hands on a rag. "'Do I contradict myself? Very well then I contradict myself.'"

Now Xavier did laugh out loud. "Whitman? Really?"

"Why not Whitman? He might actually have had a similar discussion going on in his head."

"Whether he was gay? Or whether that was even relevant? I think I'm about fifteen years past that particular discussion."

"I meant generally. Don't get fresh with me, boy."

Xavier raised both hands in a gesture of surrender. "My apologies, sir. That was uncalled for."

"Well, you have a right to be angry about how the world treated that particular discussion, as you call it. Among other things. Not that anger improves your life."

"No." Xavier sighed. "And most days I don't even think about it. But sometimes . . ." He shook his head. Being gay was not even the issue here. "Do you ever want to just grab people by the neck and tell them to get their friggin' act together? That they're wrong, and your way is actually the right way to do things? For their own good?"

His father laughed. "Oh, do I just." He grew more serious. "All the time."

"Really?" Interesting. "How do you deal with it? Just swallow it?"

"Sometimes. Depends on the situation. On whether I think telling them will start a fight or improve things."

"The subtle art of diplomacy?"

"Diplomacy, psychology, instinct." He rubbed his thumb against the tips of his fingers. "*Fingerspitzengefühl.*"

Intuition, feeling one's way through each individual situation for an appropriate reaction. Which was basically what Xavier had been doing with Doran. Like father like son? Maybe more so than Xavier had realized. He'd never thought of his father as a particularly imperious man, but he did have that quiet authority. And he knew all about difficult partnerships. Apart from Ma being as unbending as they came, interracial marriages hadn't exactly been run-of-the-mill in the seventies. No, his father knew who he was and what he wanted, and would go his own way rather than compromise his convictions. Small wonder they'd both chosen solitary professions. "Society can be a bitch."

"And is by no means always right. Society can't know you like you know yourself. So don't let society be the judge of your actions. Only you can judge you."

With that, his father went back to his workbench, and so did Xavier, turning that piece of advice over and around in his mind, and looking at it from every angle, reassured and cocooned in their shared silence.

CHAPTER FIVE

D oran flew through Sunday and Monday by focusing on what had happened Saturday night and ignoring his Sunday morning brain fart with the lottery tickets. He didn't know what had gotten into him, if he'd been testing himself or Xavier. If so, for what? He had a vague feeling it hadn't gone according to plan, but what had been the plan? He didn't want to think about it. Bottom line, he hadn't bought any lottery tickets. That was good enough.

He might have crossed his fingers in his pockets on the way to his probation meeting on Monday evening, but nothing could shake the conviction that his luck would hold.

He ran up the stairs to Elena's office, and arrived out of breath and with anticipation curling in his stomach.

Her bright smile said this was his lucky day indeed. "You're in a good mood today. Can you read my mind?"

Doran smiled back. "I'm out of the GA meeting?"

She nodded. "You are. Congratulations. I've managed to enroll you in a SMART recovery program in Port Angeles. It's a bit of a walk from the bus, but I thought you wouldn't mind."

"Not one bit." He felt like dancing in the street. Life was good. Life was excellent, in fact. "Thank you so much."

She beamed with what looked like genuine pleasure at having been able to help. "I've also made a comment on the program for future investigation."

She didn't even ask her usual questions, just gave him the address and a printed sign-in form, then told him about the program and what to expect. Apparently it focused on choice and self-reliance with face-to-face and online meetings. Doran smiled and nodded and only listened with half an ear, because fireworks were zapping through his brain. But what he did get all sounded so much better than GA.

Staring at the car lights speeding past the bus window on the way home, he wished he had Xavier's number so he could share his elation. He resolved to ask him about it the next time they met.

Because there would be a next time. Right?

The thought brought him to a desperate stop. Like drawing the last card to complete your flush and having it be the wrong color, leaving you with nothing. Xavier hadn't said anything about a next time. They'd made no plans, no date.

He was suddenly cold, and wrapped himself deeper into his hoodie, wishing it was Xavier pulling him into his open jacket. Holding him close. Making a world for just the two of them. Like the blanket forts he'd built as a child, only better.

With his head leaning against the window, he pushed the gloom aside to better imagine a life with Xavier in it. He mentally erased all the bad shit, like owing money, being kicked out, jail, and GA meetings. Then he sketched in an indulgent smile, solid arms to protect him, and a body that— Oh god, just remembering Xavier's naked body made him shift in his seat. Smooth, muscled perfection, endless legs, powerful chest. The memory of those long-fingered hands on his skin, their teasing, tormenting feather touch, had him clamp his lips shut so he wouldn't moan in the middle of the bus.

There had to be a next time. Had to. It would be too cruel to get a glimpse of something like that—something caring and safe, and yet tempting and fierce and intense—only to have it yanked away again like everything else in his life. Xavier wouldn't have invested all that planning and dinner and effort for nothing but a blowjob. Would he? But maybe he'd expected more. Would he walk away because he hadn't gotten it? Doran knew just how easy he was to walk away from. He also knew that Xavier wasn't that kind of guy. The only thing he didn't know was what had made Xavier walk toward him in the first place.

The address Elena had given him yesterday turned out to be one of those large office blocks with a whole bunch of doctor, lawyer, and architect offices sharing a lobby. It had been a half-hour walk from the bus, but while the temperature had dropped down to just above freezing, at least it wasn't raining. Doran beelined it past the information desk to the row of elevators on one side. Fourth floor, his note said.

Inside the elevator the little label next to the "4" sported the SMART Recovery® name and logo in between a *Dr. W. Jenkins, Psychologist* and a notary's office.

Up on the fourth floor, the door with the same logo was closed. Doran knocked, then, when no one answered tried the knob. Locked. He checked his watch, not quite six thirty. The meeting didn't start until seven, but he'd been asked to come early for his first time.

Across the hallway, the door to the psychologist's practice stood wide open to a reception desk, where a woman sat talking on the phone. She nodded when she saw him looking, and he turned away. When he looked again, she was gone.

A minute later, a guy in his fifties appeared in the door. His slacks, polo shirt, and tan all said money, but his smile was open, and he held out his hand when he said, "Doran, right? I'm Will Jenkins. I advise the SMART meeting when needed."

Doran shook his hand, not sure what to say to that.

"Kelly, your facilitator, should be here shortly. If you'd care to step into my office for a minute, I can fill you in on the details and give you your worksheet." Dr. Jenkins tilted his head in question, as if Doran had a choice.

Doran nodded, Xavier's easy *Lead the way* echoing in his brain. Yeah, he'd need to shut that up for the next hour and a half.

The office was medium-sized, but so crammed with bookshelves that it barely had room for the desk and a chair on each side. Dr. Jenkins indicated with a handwave that Doran should sit, and started leafing through a folder on the windowsill.

He came back with a single sheet that he handed to Doran. "This is for you to contemplate and fill in. We call it our cost–benefit analysis, which is to help you figure out what you get out of your addiction and what it costs you."

Doran nodded. "When do I have to hand it in?"

Dr. Jenkins was squeezing into the chair behind his desk, but at that he looked up. "You don't hand it in. This is for you. It's not a task to tick off. It's a tool to help you decide what direction to take, and when it gets rough, to remind you what conclusions you came to."

Doran looked at the sheet. A basic table, two rows, two columns. Advantages and disadvantages of *using or doing* at the top, and of *NOT using or NOT doing* at the bottom. Huh.

"SMART stands for Self-Management and Recovery Training. Self-management! That's you. Your choices. The group can give you the tools, but you have to use those tools. We can help and motivate, but you decide what you want to do, when you want to do it. It's your life to turn around."

This was what he'd wanted, but hearing it like that scared the shit out of him. He had a fleeting glimpse of why people might prefer the GA meetings. So much easier and less scary to put that load on someone else's shoulders. Broad ones, preferably. Xavier had held him back before. Which, he realized, was what Sunday morning at the lottery place had been about. He'd wanted Xavier to stop him. Or, at least, he'd wanted to know if he cared enough to stop him. Well, Xavier had done the stopping all right. Though it hadn't exactly sounded very caring. More like annoyed.

Maybe Xavier'd had a right to be annoyed. According to Dr. Jenkins, it was Doran himself who should be doing the stopping. But then, he'd known that, really. It was why he was here. He just didn't know how. What if he couldn't do this?

Doran crossed his fingers in his pocket. "Okay."

Dr. Jenkins looked doubtful, but he led Doran back to the meeting room, where the door was now open and a guy in his twenties, who had surfer dude written all over him, was cleaning a whiteboard. Dr. Jenkins introduced him as Kelly, and went back to his office.

Doran left Kelly to his preparations and sat in one of five chairs that had been arranged in a circle. A very small meeting, then. The room was bare except for a small bookcase under the window with magazines on top, and two framed posters on one wall. The left one read, *Resistance is not futile*, over a picture of a broken chain. The other one said, *Stretch yourself*, and showed a girl on a yoga mat.

An elderly man came in and took his seat, and right behind him a girl who looked younger than Doran, and who threw him a curious glance as she sat down. The last one was a woman in her thirties who closed the door behind herself before she sat.

"Good," Kelly said. "Since everyone's here, we might as well get started." He looked at Doran. "You're welcome to just listen until you feel comfortable. Your call. Take as much time as you need." He smiled at each of them in turn. "How has everyone been this week?"

That seemed to be their clue for something like a check-in, but there was no formula here. The girl told them how she'd gone to the library for a whole afternoon without taking her phone, which seemed to be a big deal. When she was done, she smiled at Doran. "I'm T.J., by the way."

Doran gave his name in return, but didn't volunteer anything beyond that. And just as Kelly had promised, that seemed to be perfectly fine with everyone.

The other two, Joseph and Karen, both mentioned alcohol, and Karen said she'd had no luck so far with her job application. It was a relief not to have to listen to people talk about gambling, and eye-opening to hear that others struggled with the same problems in different areas.

Then Kelly talked about how important it was to eat well and exercise and not to forget about fun activities to relieve the daily grind and to fill possible empty hours, inviting comments and input on how they were each planning their week and if they had any questions he might address at the next meeting.

That was it. When Doran checked his watch, a good hour had passed, and he'd hardly noticed.

"Do you need me to sign your attendance sheet?" Kelly asked.

"Thanks, I completely forgot about that."

"If you have access to a computer, check the website. There's some useful stuff there that'll tide you over until next week." Kelly handed him his attendance sheet back with a flyer and pointed to the URL at the bottom.

"Thanks," Doran said again. He'd have to try from the office when he was alone. Surely if there was one site worth not blocking, it was this one.

The site was indeed not blocked, and Doran browsed through the given info and watched the introduction video during his lunch hour over the next couple of days. But none of it really stuck in his brain. Not hearing anything from Xavier was keeping him off-balance, and his thoughts went around in circles with reasons why Xavier would or wouldn't walk away.

It wasn't until Friday that he pulled out the worksheet Dr. Jenkins had given him. It seemed a little stupid. Advantages and disadvantages of doing? As in gambling? Hello, Captain Obvious. *WIN*, he put in bold letters at the top left, and *LOSE* on the other side. The not doing part was harder. He shoved the sheet back into his notebook. Drummed his fingers on the desk. He could go out. Just to get a sandwich. No more lottery tickets. Though, did the promise still count if Xavier never showed up again?

But he would. It wasn't the weekend yet. Not quite. On Sunday he'd be at the gas station, and Doran could go over and talk to him. Easy. He wasn't a stranger anymore, after all.

For now, though, he'd better get back to work. He did a last read through his newsletter file, submitted it to the director for review, then got up to get himself a coffee.

A shadow at the door made him jump. Xavier. The joy bubbling up inside him made it easy to ignore the trepidation, which he didn't have a reason for anyway.

He went to open the door, and Xavier's low, gravelly "Hey" raised expectant goose bumps on his skin.

"Hey yourself."

"You said you could take some time off during the week." Xavier came in and leaned against the door from the inside.

Doran's heart did funny things in his throat. "Like now?"

"Like now."

"I'll just have to shut everything down and lock up."

When he didn't move, Xavier turned him around by the shoulders. "Go do it, then."

Doran did as he was told, and only when they sat in Xavier's truck did he ask, "Where are we going?"

"I want to show you the park. Well, a view of it. You said you'd never been there." Xavier threw him a quick glance. "Over dinner the other night."

"Oh, yeah. No. I know." Why did this man always scramble his brain? Maybe because he always did the unexpected, catching Doran off guard. Like suggesting an afternoon in the park on an overcast day in March.

He watched Xavier's hands on the wheel, then his profile, lit up occasionally by the sun peeking through the clouds. He hadn't been paying attention to where they were going and was surprised when Xavier slowed and hooked a right just before Joyce. Midday light turned as dark as dusk among the trees.

Doran started to fidget in the continued silence. "Don't you have to work today?"

"I took the afternoon off."

They crossed a couple of creeks or small rivers, then Xavier slowed again and turned left. A parking lot and low-slung building came into view, and suddenly they were out of the forest and on the shore of a lake.

"Where are we?"

"At the northern shore of Lake Crescent."

Xavier stopped the truck, shrugging into his jacket as he got out. Doran was starting to get used to the fact that he was expected to follow without explanation. He pulled both his hoods and the zippers up and got out of the truck.

A thin mist hung over the water, and the tops of the mountains on the lake's other side were covered by fog or low clouds. The air even tasted of fog, and maybe snow. Cleaner somehow. Doran took a deep gulp of it.

In a low voice Xavier pointed out directions and places. Doran wasn't listening because he was preoccupied with the way Xavier's cheek muscles moved. He wanted his sketch pad for both landscapes: the trees-and-lake one as well as the skin-and-bones one.

Now and then the cloud cover parted and a weak sun shone through and reflected off the water.

Doran suddenly realized that Xavier had fallen silent and was watching him.

"It's so quiet," Doran said. "Doesn't anyone come here?"

"Not outside the season."

Xavier studied the path running along the shoreline, then said, "Do you have sturdier shoes?"

Doran looked at his sneakers. "Afraid not."

"Too bad. I can't take you hiking in those. That is, do you even hike?"

"Dunno, never have." The cold started to creep under Doran's clothes, and he shivered.

Xavier stepped behind him, and Doran held his breath when he heard the zipper open, then he was indeed wrapped in that jacket again. *Oh god, yes please.* He closed his eyes and let his head fall back against Xavier's shoulder. Best place in the world. "I wasn't sure if I'd see you again."

"Why not?"

"You didn't say anything."

Xavier held him tight and gently kissed his temple. "Exactly. Disappearing without a word would have been a rather rude move." He paused. "Is that how you see me?"

"No! Oh god, no. Just, it's not like I'm . . . I mean, what does someone like you want with someone like me?"

Xavier let him go and turned him around. "What is that supposed to mean?"

Wasn't it obvious? Doran avoided his eyes, looking at Xavier's shoes instead, thick-soled hiking boots. "It's okay," he mumbled. "You don't have to be nice about it."

Xavier turned him again, pointing out over Doran's shoulder at the lake. Solid muscle at his back, a whisper of air against his cheek when he said, "That surface of the water, blue gray with clouds and mist, with flashes of blue where the sun hits it? Deep and changeable, and you could look at it for hours without getting bored? That's what your eyes are like."

Xavier hugged him close, back against chest and wrapped his jacket around him again. He had smoothed Doran's double hood back, and his lips were brushing Doran's ear when he murmured, "Your lashes paint shadows on your cheeks when you sleep, and I have a permanent desire to kiss your eyebrows."

Doran closed his eyes, strangely centered and completely still inside. He would like to draw the person Xavier was describing. That wasn't him. Not really. Xavier seeing that in him was a wispy miracle, like the seed head of a dandelion. He didn't dare breathe for fear of having it disintegrate. But then Xavier's lips wandered down his neck, and Doran, lowering his head to give him more access, drew a deep, shuddering breath. Delicious goose bumps sprang up all along his arms and back.

He felt Xavier's hand move down his chest and stomach and, ever so slowly, across the front of his jeans, which grew tight in response. Xavier kept his hand there, Doran could feel the heat of it through the fabric, then Xavier curved his fingers and drew his nails across Doran's now perfectly hard cock, sending flashes of agonizing pleasure through his body.

Xavier kissed his jaw right below the ear and growled, "Don't you dare come in your pants."

Of course that instantly jacked up Doran's need to come right now to desperation level.

Xavier pressed the heel of his hand against Doran's hard-on and pushed down along the length of it, then repeated the upward motion with his nails.

Doran couldn't suppress a whimper.

"Don't even think about it." He could hear the smile in Xavier's voice. The bastard was enjoying this. Inexplicably that turned him on even more.

"Maybe we should take this to your place," Xavier said.

What the . . .? "That's an almost forty-five-minute drive."

"Yeees?" Definitely a soft laugh in there now.

"I'll never last that long."

"Well, I'm not having sex in the car. So, you'll have to figure something out. Unless . . ."

"Unless what?" Doran gasped.

Xavier straightened up behind him. Throwing him back on himself. *Nonono.*

"My place is close, but it's in the middle of nowhere."

"So?"

"So, you want to go with a guy you hardly know to his house in the boonies? Don't you watch horror movies?"

"I'm in the boonies now," Doran said desperately. Why were they having this discussion? Why now? "And I'm not with just any guy; I'm with you."

Doran couldn't tell if that was a hitched breath or a huff of laughter behind him. He turned. "Are you planning to hurt me?"

The amusement in Xavier's eyes died and was replaced by the same look that had caressed Doran in the restaurant. "No, I'm planning not to hurt you."

"See? Can we go now? To your place?"

For a second Doran thought Xavier would say no, but then he cupped Doran's cheek and kissed the spot between his eyebrows. "Very well, then."

Doran sighed in relief and beelined back to the truck, climbing in carefully, to avoid any excess chafing in his pants. He needed to calm down. Which, with Xavier giving him a look that said he knew exactly what was going on, wasn't going to happen.

He sat on the edge of the seat and leaned his shoulders against the back.

"Seat belt," Xavier said.

Doran bit his lip, scooted a bit more upright, and fastened his seat belt. He wanted to jack off so badly, it almost hurt.

"If you come in your pants," Xavier said, "I'm going to drive you straight home and leave you there."

Bastard. For a terrifying second, Doran wasn't sure whether he'd said that out loud. He threw Xavier a quick look, but the ranger was checking the mirror, backing the car out of the lot.

Doran leaned his head against the seat and grabbed the edges of the cushion to keep his hands by his sides. This would be one hell of an agonizing ride. Unfortunately the thought didn't soften his hard-on the least little bit. Quite the opposite, in fact.

He wasn't paying attention to the little roads they were taking, but it wasn't as long as he'd feared before Xavier stopped the truck.

When they got out, Doran had a brief impression of a log cabin in the gathering dusk, but he was too focused on Xavier and on the way he moved to do much looking around.

And then they were inside, Doran had a wall at his back and Xavier's lips on his, and Xavier's hands in his hair and under his shirt, roaming all over his body at will, pinching his nipples, sliding into his pants to grab his ass, stripping him naked. Then his bare ass hit the table, and the hands pushed him back, sending waves of longing agony through his body, and sweeping away fears and insecurities in a rush of need to give himself up to this man who made him feel safe and wanted and whole.

CHAPTER SIX

X avier grabbed the back of Doran's knees and pulled his feet up over his shoulders, so Doran's shoulders hit the table. He pressed his crotch against Doran's buttocks, half expecting scared surprise, and ready to break off. But all he got was a moan of pleasure and Doran grabbing the edges of the table he was lying on. *Hot damn.* He pushed Doran's knees down toward his chest. "Hold on to your legs."

When Doran did, he skimmed his knuckles over Doran's buttock and balls, which elicited another low moan. He took a step back to enjoy the view.

"Imagine I'm touching you."

A harsh inhale, then, "Where?"

"Anywhere you want."

A quiver ran through Doran's thigh muscles, and Xavier's pants grew uncomfortably tight.

He went over to the bed to get the bottle of lube. Doran's stomach rose and fell with quick, shallow breaths.

Xavier stripped and lubed himself up. "You don't come without permission." He squeezed some more lube into his hand and spread it over Doran's cock, watching his stomach muscles spasm.

"Oh god, please. I'm so close."

"Focus."

Xavier wrapped his hand around both their cocks and started a loose-fisted stroke that had Doran whimpering as if he were being tortured. He held on to his legs, but spread them wider to give Xavier better access. His eyes were closed; his lips moved with unspoken pleas. A thin sheen of sweat appeared on his skin, despite the coolness of the air, and his brows drew together in that frown of concentration Xavier loved. He was beyond gorgeous.

"Please Xavier, I can't, can't hold back—"

"You can and you will." He was getting close himself. On the next upstroke he drew his thumb across the tops of their cocks.

Doran gave a shout and his eyes flew open, his pupils so wide that they looked black.

Xavier groaned. Nothing, nothing in the world was as much of a turn-on as those reactions. He closed his fist tighter and sped up his rhythm. Doran made a strangled sound. Xavier's balls pulled up in response and with a growl he came all over his own hand and Doran's stomach. "Now," he breathed, "you can come."

He didn't even get to finish the sentence before Doran came with two, three full-body jerks that slowly subsided to smaller spasms.

Xavier reached for a tea towel to wipe them both dry, then dropped it on the floor, gathered Doran up in his arms, and carried him over to the bed to gather him snug into the curve of his body.

He could feel Doran's heart hammering against his palm. "That's what you get for coming to the cabin in the woods."

Doran huffed a laugh, still fighting for air. "Was that supposed to teach me a lesson?"

"Sass, huh? Duly noted."

Another weak laugh answered him, but Xavier could already feel Doran's muscles relax into sleep.

He watched Doran sleep for a while, then gently extracted his arm from under Doran's head, careful not to wake him, and got up. His stomach reminded him that he'd missed dinner. He pulled on his pants and a sweater and padded over to the kitchen. Armed with a sandwich and a mug of tea, he installed himself at his desk to enter the latest fisher sightings into the map. But instead, hands wrapped around the mug, he caught himself staring out the window at the tree tops moving against the moonlit clouds.

Doran blew him away, and the longer he was around him the more impossible it became to let him go. Doran was giving him something he hadn't even known he'd wanted, the trust of near-total surrender. And he hadn't known he had what Doran was so obviously looking for: to be claimed beyond reason or awareness. But now that he knew, he couldn't stop wanting it. And he was increasingly questioning why he should try.

He wasn't hurting Doran. On the contrary, Xavier taking over calmed Doran down. He was always asking for it, actively and implicitly. And tonight, when Doran had looked downright transported, it felt so perfect that he couldn't believe what he was doing was wrong. Then why couldn't he get rid of that uneasy niggle in the back of his mind?

He hadn't been straight enough for his church, nor black enough for some of his classmates in college, but the scandalized whispers hadn't made him straight, nor had being called an Oreo made him hide his upbringing. All those had ever done was to make him walk his own road.

He didn't know what they would call him now, and he didn't care. Not about what others thought. His own thoughts were a different story, though. He needed to be convinced that he was doing the right thing. Accepting Doran's surrender required a heightened level of trust, and Xavier wasn't sure they were there yet. So far Doran hadn't indicated any boundaries, and Xavier was reluctant to find them by pushing harder, because he couldn't decide if Doran was amazingly astute, heedless, or downright self-destructive.

A rustle behind him made him swivel in his chair. Doran was stretching his arms above his head, then got up and wrapped the blanket around himself like a cape.

"Are you cold? I normally make a fire when I get home, but I got . . . sidetracked." Xavier grinned. "There's bread and stuff on the table if you're hungry."

Doran came toward him, straddled his legs, and sat on his knees. *Hot damn.*

"I could eat." But instead he slung his arms around Xavier's neck and kissed him.

Xavier leaned back and, grabbing Doran's buttocks, hitched him up higher without breaking the kiss. They were both getting hard just fooling around in the chair.

He got up with Doran still wrapped around him and gently deposited him in the chair. "Food."

Doran looked like he was going to protest, but then he merely pulled the blanket more tightly around himself.

Xavier made a second sandwich, and when he came back to the desk, Doran was studying the map. "Where are we on that?"

Xavier tapped the screen. "We're right here."

"So your house is inside the park? Cool."

"Yup. Technically, this is an old guard station, but I've fixed up at least the roof so many damn times that I'm sure none of it is original anymore."

Doran took the sandwich and made room for Xavier to sit again, then sat on his lap. He looked at the maps and official notices on the walls and the corkboard, then at the radio on the desk. "It doubles as your office?"

"It does. It's also an emergency shelter, but I don't get a lot of people out here."

"It's small for all that."

Xavier tried to see the one-room blockhouse through Doran's eyes. "I suppose. But I don't need much inside space." He'd thought of partitioning off the kitchen a few years back, but the woodstove was the only source of heat, so he'd left it. The only thing he'd added was the bathroom, because the original structure had only had an outhouse and no shower.

Doran nodded at the lamp. "Where do you get your power?"

"From a creek behind the house. It doesn't provide enough wattage to run things like an electric stove or furnace, but it's enough for lights, a small fridge, and the stereo."

"And the computer."

Xavier nodded.

"Internet?"

"No coverage. You might get a cell phone signal on one of the mountain tops, but not down here."

"No internet at all? TV?"

Xavier laughed and shook his head. "Barbaric, isn't it?"

"Downright savage."

Xavier stood him on his feet, got up, and took the empty plate from him. "I'll have to think of something else to keep you entertained."

Doran opened the blanket wide. "I'm sure you can think of something."

Deep breath, Xavier. "You're pretty cocky." He turned to set the plate in the sink and to maintain some control.

"You gonna do something about that?"

Well, hello, provocation. "Come here."

He waited until Doran had taken the few steps, the blanket forgotten on the chair, then said, "Undress me."

There was the held breath and slight widening of eyes Xavier had been hoping for. Doran closed the gap between their bodies and, never taking his eyes off Xavier's, ran his hands under Xavier's sweater, pushing it up and leaving a trail of fire on his ribs. Xavier pulled it over his head and tossed it in the general direction of the chair.

Without looking down, Doran skittered his fingers to the waistband of Xavier's pants, popped the button, and, ever so slowly, opened the zipper. Xavier gritted his teeth. He hadn't bothered with underwear for his brief stint at the computer, and the tickling light touch was seductive torment. Doran moved his hands into Xavier's pants and over his ass cheeks, and pressed his naked body against Xavier's cock, the smoke eyes deep and faraway.

If he wasn't careful, he'd fall into those eyes, his self-control flying apart like clouds in a storm. "Bed. Now," he hissed.

Doran complied, but slowly, making every step a sinuous performance.

Xavier got rid of his pants and followed with a growl in his throat that seemed to shiver up Doran's limbs and spill out in a dreamy smile. *Holy shit.* He covered Doran's body with his, half touching, half suspended on hands and knees, nipping at bits of skin and swallowing the deep kisses Doran offered him without reserve. *Losing it, Xavier.*

Mustering every thread of discipline he possessed, he broke the kiss and rolled onto his back, pulse knocking in his throat.

Doran hitched himself up on one elbow, a faint question mark between his mobile brows. He brushed his hand across Xavier's ribcage and played with his nipple, then, when Xavier didn't say anything, straddled him and kissed his sternum. He threw Xavier a look from under his lashes and, with a saucy grin, scooted lower, placing a trail of kisses on Xavier's stomach. He licked around the navel, then followed the treasure trail with his tongue.

Xavier held his breath when Doran pressed his face against his cock. Warm tongue, cool air. Xavier scrunched up the pillow behind his neck so he could watch Doran's lips close around his cock, the visual enhancing the sensation and vice versa. He tried to relax even as his pulse sped up again. Now and then Doran threw him a glance as if to ask if what he was doing was okay, and every time those storm-cloud eyes met his, Xavier felt it in his ass and down the back of his thighs. The muscles in his abdomen tightened when Doran closed his hand around the shaft, adding pressure to the slick movement of his mouth. Xavier groaned and thought he saw a smile in Doran's eyes, when he sped up his perfect rhythm, acknowledged the fracture lines running through his own composure as the pressure built deep inside. "Yes. That's good. That's . . . very good."

The familiar tingle in his balls, muscles contracting. "I'm going to come." But Doran kept going, sending lightning surges from Xavier's ass to his toes. Xavier pried his hand loose from the sheet to push Doran away, but the heat of his mouth vanished at the last second, only his hand continuing its movement in time with the waves of dizzy release racing through Xavier's body.

Doran's head came to rest on his hip, and Xavier threaded his fingers through the silk of his hair, savoring the sleepy relaxation trickling into his muscles. He was aware of Doran wiping the cum from his stomach, then pulling himself up and snuggling into Xavier's shoulder, tugging the duvet over them both.

The moon threw a shadow of the window's transom on Doran's shoulder and made his skin seem luminous. His muscles relaxed against Xavier's body, and his breathing evened as he drifted off to sleep. Xavier wasn't far behind.

He woke up in the dark, and rolled out of bed, shivering in the cold air. Doran mumbled something in his sleep and moved into the body-warm spot. Xavier stuffed the blankets tight around his spare frame and went to start a fire.

Holding his hands out, he stared into the flames as the kindling caught. The woodbox was almost empty. He nudged the two smallish pieces that were left into the fire and closed the stove door, then took the box and a flashlight, stepped into his shoes, and went outside. The air was clammy with early morning drizzle, little droplets of which caught in his lashes and beaded on his skin as he filled the box and hauled it back inside. He kicked his shoes off, added more wood, and closed the stove again, moving on automatic, the sleep fog refusing to lift. He waited just long enough to make sure the fire wasn't doing anything funny, then crawled back into bed.

"You're cold," Doran said without opening his eyes.

"Shhh, go back to sleep." He pulled Doran on top of his body for warmth, but also because he was taking all the space.

"I am asleep," Doran said against his chest.

The next time he woke, the sky outside was light, and his arm felt dead. He gently tugged it out from under Doran's head and flexed his hand to get the blood moving again.

"Sorry," Doran mumbled, only half-awake.

Xavier sat up and rubbed the sleep out of his eyes. The cabin was pleasantly warm now. He got up to stoke the fire, throw another log on, and set a pot of water on the stove for coffee.

Doran had propped himself up on one elbow, watching him.

"What?"

"You are so stunning."

The way Doran looked at him was quickly making him forget about coffee. If he was going to get anything done today, to say nothing of getting Doran into work on time, he should probably put some pants on. "I'll be in the shower. I'll make it quick to leave you some warm water. Just remember there's not a lot of it, or you'll end up with cold."

Doran's grin said he hadn't missed what he was doing to Xavier and he enjoyed it. *Little shit.*

He got another look when he came out of the shower and Doran walked past him for his turn. Downright coy this one, upwards from under the veil of lashes.

"You watch it, boy," he growled.

He saw the shiver run through Doran's body at that. *Damn. Breakfast, Xavier.*

He got eggs and butter out of the minifridge he ran on the creek generator, and set a skillet on the stove, then quickly got dressed.

He couldn't decide whether Doran was deliberately baiting him, or if they were just so well-matched in what they wanted that they unconsciously pulled in the same direction. Maybe a bit of both. He certainly wasn't hard to bait these days. The longer they were together, the more easily they fell into these roles of . . . what, exactly? He still didn't know what Doran got out of it, other than it obviously turned him on. Maybe that was all that mattered. But it didn't help him define the strange power dynamic that was developing between them, at least not on a cognitive level. His instincts seemed to have a better idea of it.

He cut the butter into the now hot skillet and watched it melt and foam.

So far those instincts had proven good; maybe he should push a bit more to find Doran's limits. And to tease out what he was holding back. Like aspects of that gambling addiction. Yeah, time to see how much Doran was willing to talk about. If nothing else, it might give Xavier a better idea of where he stood and how many secrets the boy was keeping.

As if on cue, Doran came back from his shower, bare-ass naked.

Xavier ignored him, set up the coffee pot, got out plates, and cracked the eggs into the butter.

"Is it very different, cooking on a woodstove?"

Xavier ran a spatula along the edges of the eggs to loosen them and loaded two slices of bread into the camp toaster. "The cooking itself is not that different. The main difficulty is getting the temperature you want and keeping it even. That takes a bit more time than turning a knob."

"Will you show me?"

"Are you planning on getting a woodstove?"

Doran studied his bare toes, then tilted his head, giving Xavier a shy look, his eyebrows cocked at an irresolute, and utterly kissable, angle. "Maybe I'd like to cook breakfast for you next time?" The way his voice rose a fraction at the end made it sound like a question. A slew of questions in fact. *Will you let me cook? Will there be a next time? Is this a relationship? Heading where exactly?*

Those last two Xavier would like to get an answer to himself. He tore his gaze away from the embodiment of temptation in front of him and checked on the coffee. "Go dress. Breakfast is almost ready."

He poured coffee and brought everything over to the table, then sat, facing Doran. "Tell me about gambling."

Doran sputtered into his mug. "What?"

"How did you get started?"

There was a hesitant pause before Doran mumbled into his cup, "My dad used to take me to the races on Sunday mornings, when Mom was at church. Back before she made everyone go." He looked up at the window, obviously seeing something different than the trees outside. "We'd each pick a horse and bet five bucks on it." Xavier got a shy grin. "We were lousy at picking winners."

"So, what's the draw today?"

"Duh, still winning."

"Really. With lottery tickets. How disappointing, I thought you were smarter than that."

Doran pulled the yolk of his egg apart with a strip of toast. "Fine. So maybe it's not about the money."

"About what, then?"

The yolk ran slowly across his plate, apparently fascinating Doran no end. "It's exciting. And it makes me feel good," he finally said. "Poker's better for that, though. I'm not constantly thinking about stuff when I'm playing. About what I want and can't have, what I shouldn't, what I am. You know? Stuff."

The answer gave Xavier a sinking feeling in the pit of his stomach. "Yeees?"

Doran shrugged and looked at Xavier with something very close to a challenge in his eyes. "Beats drinking?"

Xavier nodded slowly, chewing on his piece of toast. He understood some of that, especially the *what I want, what I shouldn't* part. At least in what other people thought he shouldn't. Be gay, like classical music, live in the woods for the rest of his life . . . Yeah, he'd been there. Though maybe not quite to the point of desperation he saw flickering in Doran's eyes. "Okay." He watched Doran wipe the yolk off his plate with the rest of his toast. "So, how do you get out of that . . . need?"

Doran brought his plate over to the sink and rinsed it, then leaned against the counter. "There are programs. The first one I was in, Gamblers Anonymous, sucked. At least for me. I was really lucky to get out of that. The new one I just started seems better, despite this stupid questioning sheet. Dunno yet." The look he sent Xavier, half don't-touch-me, half puppy-in-need-of-a-home, didn't help with the sinking feeling at all.

"Doran, you're not just trying to replace one set of feel-good excitement or distraction with another from me, are you?"

The don't-touch-me look won for a second. "Nothing wrong with that." Then the hopeful puppy was back. "Not if you want it too."

Xavier's deep breath came out more like a sigh. He didn't feel ready for a deeper evaluation of his disappointment about being just a distraction, for this whole discussion really, but it was needed. He needed it. To sort this out and make sure.

He shook his head. "I don't deny that whatever game we've been playing can be hot as hell. But games can't replace life. I don't believe you can live your life filled with nothing but excitement and distraction. If you never take responsibility for anything, it'll stay empty. And you can't give that responsibility up to me either. Ultimately, giving it up to anything would cripple you. It's already hurt you. That's not what I want out of this." He covered the space between them with a wave of his hand across the table. "Is that what you want?"

He was almost glad Doran didn't answer. He didn't think that whatever was between them would have survived a yes.

"That 'stupid questionnaire sheet.' Do you have it with you?"

The quick, furtive look toward the backpack by the wall was all the answer Xavier needed. *Don't lie to me now, kid.*

"Yes."

"Show me?"

The range of expressions Doran's eyebrows were capable of displaying endlessly fascinated Xavier. The current one was downright sullen. Nevertheless Doran went to his backpack, pulled a single sheet out, and handed it to Xavier. A simple enough decision guide, positives and negatives of gambling or quitting. Xavier stared at the words *win* and *lose* Doran had scribbled at the top, then at Doran.

He didn't even know where to start explaining how much crap that was. Especially after Doran had just told him that it wasn't about the money.

Then Doran's eyes shifted away. He knew. The little shit knew that what he'd written was a cop-out. He'd managed to get into the program he'd wanted, and now he was going to blow it? Xavier wanted to shake him and hug him at the same time. He could see all that potential locked down in hang-ups and insecurities, and it drove him nuts that he had no idea how to break through them.

Well, it couldn't be forced. Maybe the best he could do was not reward it. Plus, some quiet reflection would do them both good.

He gritted his teeth and handed the sheet back. "You know this is bull. You just told me as much."

Doran made no move to take it. "If you know everything so much better, why don't you fill it out?"

Xavier counted silently to ten so he wouldn't start yelling. "You can't escape taking charge of your life. I need to know that you can take care of yourself. That you *will* take care of yourself."

Doran didn't answer. He took the sheet back and stashed it.

"Damn it, Doran, you can't just shrug it off. I'm not going to let this go. I'll ask you again tonight. At least show me that you tried."

Still he didn't get an answer. Well, he'd know soon enough if Doran had heard him. "C'mon. I'd better get you into town, or you'll be late for work."

That night he deliberately waited until after six before driving around to the Tourist Information to pick Doran up. He'd meant it when he'd said to give the sheet some serious thought. So he wasn't about to provide Doran with any excuses by showing up too early.

Doran opened the door so quickly when Xavier knocked that he must have been waiting to let him in.

Xavier locked back up from the inside, and when he turned around, Doran was kneeling in front of him, eyes downcast, holding out a condom like an offering on his flat palm. The view and its implication sent every available drop of Xavier's blood south. Christ, that was unexpected. He didn't remember what he'd been thinking.

He threw a quick glance at the way-too-visible storefront window, then nodded toward the back of the office. "We're not going to turn up on any security video, are we? I really don't want to get you fired."

Doran shook his head. "Not in the break room." He led the way to a windowless room with a coffeemaker and small fridge. Four steel-and-plastic chairs huddled around a kitchen table, and an upholstered office chair had been rolled into a corner.

Xavier sat in the office chair, hands on the armrests. He leaned back and let his legs fall open.

Doran immediately went back down on his knees between Xavier's feet. No questions, no protest that he'd maybe expected something else. He bent forward and followed the now very visible outline of Xavier's cock with his nose, then his lips. *Hot damn.*

He tongued the zipper and pulled it down with his teeth, throwing Xavier a smoldering look from under his lashes that set Xavier's thighs tingling. Doran popped the button on Xavier's pants, and Xavier shifted in his seat to allow him to strip his briefs off. Xavier's cock slapped against his abdomen, sending up a spike of arousal that seemed to have pierced his lungs, because breathing became quite difficult.

Doran splayed both hands on Xavier's stomach, then licked his balls and shaft with flat, massaging strokes. The rising tension in Xavier's muscles forced a groan up his throat. He threaded his fingers through Doran's hair, pushing the bangs back from his face, so he wouldn't miss any of the emotions playing out there.

Doran had his eyes closed and seemed lost in what he was doing. His hand moved down and closed around Xavier's cock, bringing the tip to his lips. He gave a couple more licks, then took him in as deeply as he could and started to suck. It took every ounce of control Xavier had left not to push his head down all the way. He let the arousal kick into his muscles, but kept his hips perfectly still and let Doran do whatever he wanted, only smoothing his hair back now and then. Doran used lips and tongue and his hand in perfect combination, but it was the rapt expression on his face that really got to Xavier. He looked as though he'd never enjoyed anything as much as Xavier's cock in his mouth.

It tightened every muscle in Xavier's body, and he found himself decidedly short of breath when he said, "Now's a good time to use that condom."

With a faint look of regret Doran leaned back, fished the condom out of his pocket and ripped it open, then rolled it on, slowly and with an air of concentration that turned the simple act into something akin to worship. He carefully smoothed down the sides with his fingertips, then made a fist above the little roll at the end. He deliberately held eye contact when he closed his lips over Xavier's cock again, swirled his tongue around the tip, then sucked him in and, matching the movement with his hand, set a slightly faster rhythm than before.

The tension deep inside Xavier's body unraveled into little zings of electricity that ran through his buttocks and thighs, down to his toes. His balls pulled up tight, and as much as he wanted to watch Doran's face, he couldn't keep his eyes open when the first wave hit him. His body jerked in the chair, and his head banged against the wall behind him. But the moan he heard wasn't his. He could feel it reverberate around his cock and intensify the tingling pulses that bled out the tension into the profound relief of his release.

For a moment he just sat there with Doran's head resting on his thigh, not trusting himself to move, savoring the languid repleteness of his muscles.

When he raised his head, Doran slid the condom off and knotted it up, then ever so gently pulled Xavier's briefs back up and closed his pants. "I was daydreaming about this all day long," he said with a blissful little smile.

"You must've gotten an awful lot of work done."

Doran grinned as he got up and disposed of the condom. Xavier had a brief flash of the face of the next person opening that trash can, and hoped they wouldn't look too closely.

Pushing himself out of the chair felt like his body had gained at least twenty pounds over the last ten minutes or so.

He pulled Doran close and kissed him deeply, tasting his own skin and the latex. Conquered by the way Doran melted into his body, kissing him back with a mix of hunger and reverence that hit his veins like a drug.

When he had to come up for air, he smoothed Doran's hair back and drank in the beauty of his eyes, his cheekbones, even that stubborn chin. "Thank you. That was the most spectacular welcome anyone has ever given me."

Doran's smile lit up not only his eyes, but his whole face. "I'll have to do it again, then."

Xavier laughed. "You won't hear me complain. Though right now we should probably get out of here and find something to eat. For some reason I'm starving."

Doran snuggled into his arm and looked up at him. "Can we just get a pizza or something and go back to your place?"

"You want to get back into the boonies with no internet and hardly enough hot water for two showers?"

"Please?" How Doran managed to infuse his whole body with supplication, Xavier would never know.

"Well, if that's what you want, it's fine by me."

"Everything is so quiet there," Doran said dreamily.

It was one of the qualities Xavier cherished about his home, but he was surprised to hear it from Doran. He was also not entirely sure whether Doran was talking about absent traffic noises or something else. Well, he wasn't going to argue.

During the whole drive back into the park, Doran sat with his head relaxed against the seat, hands by his sides, no fidgets, no quick glances darting here and there.

Xavier studied his profile as much as the road allowed. The willful chin, the strong lines of his jawbone. It made him want to see Doran's jaw muscles tighten in an effort to keep it together. He shivered. *Road. Right.*

It was a miracle that he made it back to the cabin without driving into any trees. By the time they got out of the truck, he was holding himself on such a tight leash that he didn't trust himself to speak. He swallowed hard and tried to breathe some give into his muscles. One hand on the door, the other around the back of Doran's neck, he maneuvered them both inside, then leaned against the closing door.

At least this time he'd had the foresight to have a fire going in the stove. Just in case.

"Strip."

Despite his harsh intake of breath, Doran didn't hesitate and was out of his clothes in five seconds flat, his cock hard and jutting away from his body like a fox's tail. *Jesus.* Xavier shoved both hands into his pockets and pressed his shoulders to the door. "Turn. Slowly."

The half light of dusk carved delicious shadows into Doran's perfect leg muscles, the concave dips in his ass cheeks, the shallow navel, the hollows above his collarbones. He had his eyes closed as he performed one full rotation around his own axis.

"I didn't say you could stop," Xavier growled.

A tremor ran through Doran's body and a small bead glistened at the tip of his cock when he started to turn again.

"Christ, the things I could do to you," Xavier hissed through his teeth.

With something between a sob and a whimper Doran sank to his knees with his eyes still closed. "Please," he whispered.

Xavier nearly came. He wrapped his hand around the keys in his pocket, hard, letting the pain distract him.

Thoughts of tying him to the bed and pounding him into the mattress fought their way to the surface, only to be resolutely wrestled back down. He realized those thoughts had been lurking at the edges of his consciousness for some time. But this was Doran, the guy with no boundaries. If he ever wanted to let go of his keys again, he needed to know that the boy had some sense of self-preservation. "I'd need to be sure—" He cleared his throat because his voice sounded as if he'd dined on rusty iron. "Not unless I'm sure you know your limits. And are willing to call them. I need to be able to trust you."

Doran lowered his head. His voice was still quiet, but Xavier heard the disappointment in it anyway. "You want proof. Trust doesn't require proof. Isn't that the point? Jumping blind? That's why it's called a 'leap' of faith."

"No." Xavier tried to keep his voice level, and the rising anger born of frustration helped him focus. "Different concept. That's what I've been trying to tell you. Trust may not require constant proof, but it does need to be built. It's based in experience. It's the solid, reliable bedrock of a relationship. A leap of faith has nothing to do with that. Quite the opposite, in fact. You need to leap when, instead of a foundation and a floor, there's nothing but a hole. That leap can break your neck."

"A relationship?" Doran had raised his head, but in the fading light Xavier couldn't read his expression.

He banged the back of his head against the door. Trust the little punk to zero in on what Xavier had not wanted to say. "When you got into my truck that first day; later, when you let me into your apartment; and last night, when you agreed to come with me to the literal cabin in the woods, you risked your neck."

Doran was shaking his head. "I know what a predator looks like, okay? You're not it. Your whole argument proves my point. Stop treating me like a child."

Xavier hammered his fist against the door, which made Doran jump. "Then stop acting like one."

Doran hugged himself, but his chin jutted out when he said, "Make me."

"Goddamn it." He took a step forward and closed his hands around Doran's throat. "Do you know how little effort it would cost me to break your neck?"

A shiver ran through Doran's body, but he got to his feet against the pressure of Xavier's hands. Up close his eyes blazed with defiance. "I know exactly what it would cost you. Everything."

He was right, of course. So maybe he wasn't quite as naive as Xavier had thought. He took a deep breath. Was that enough? He ran his thumbs up Doran's throat. Doran followed the lead by tilting his chin up and closing his eyes. Yielding again as if he hadn't just butted heads with Xavier.

"I know what I want," Doran said, without opening his eyes. "Do you?"

That he wasn't looking at Xavier took the sting out of his challenge, but it made Xavier bristle, nonetheless. Wasn't that what he wanted Doran to do, though? Stand his ground when Xavier pushed him too far? It wasn't in the area Xavier had been looking for, but that shouldn't matter. Was the little shit right, then? Maybe Xavier *had* been projecting his own boundaries, his own guilt about the

control he was assuming. A control that went against every taboo about power inequality he'd ever been taught and internalized. Had he hoped Doran would tell him no, so he'd have a reason to avoid this terrifying, seductive, and uncharted territory? *Shit.*

"I like your hands around my throat," Doran whispered. "I know you're not going to choke me, and I don't want you to, but I do like it." His voice had a pleading quality now, and he was still rock-hard in the fading light.

Jesus Christ. Xavier ached to give in, give him what he wanted. What they both wanted. In the end, this was a question of choices, and if Doran wanted to give some of his choices up to him until further notice, that, too, was a choice. Who was he to deny that? But he also needed to keep him safe. And himself sane.

Over the years, self-control had become so much second nature to him that he'd forgotten how desperately elusive it could be. And yet it had never been more important not to lose it. Fuck the guilt, but this part he'd have to figure out, somehow. He'd have to watch himself as closely as Doran. Maybe more so.

He moved his hand around the back of Doran's neck and guided him toward the bed.

CHAPTER SEVEN

C ool air on his skin, and cool sheets, and Xavier murmuring half-heard things in his ear.

Doran lay prone on the mattress, with Xavier's warm, naked body half covering him, Xavier kissing his shoulder and back, running one hand up the inside of his leg, grazing his balls, and skimming up between his buttocks.

Xavier turned away for a moment, then the fingers were back, slick and insistent. Without thinking, Doran spread his legs wider. He didn't have a lot of experience with getting fucked, and the one time he'd let it happen had been . . . rough.

It would be different this time, wouldn't it? With Xavier it would be. He didn't want him to stop. The pleasure radiating through his body from the way Xavier massaged his buttocks said it would be different.

But the memory made him hesitate for a second, and Xavier noticed immediately. "Have you done this before?"

Doran tried to wrap his brain around something as complicated as speech. "Oh, yeah."

Xavier flipped him on his back and held his wrists above his head. His other hand went between Doran's legs and continued what it had been doing, his wrist grazing Doran's balls, making him pull his knees up.

"Yeah?" With that, one of Xavier's fingers was inside him, and it felt much bigger than it should have. Doran opened his eyes and looked straight into Xavier's, which were filled with teasing amusement.

"You're an expert, in fact."

Doran's brain was too busy processing all the different sensations that Xavier's fingers—there was definitely more than one now—sent through his body to guard what he should say. "Only once."

His instinct was to give himself up to whatever Xavier wanted to do to him. Only Xavier was making him wait. The more Xavier played, the more pleasure overtook discomfort. And the more frustrating the waiting got. He wanted to come so badly that it threw out any other thought.

But his wrists were trapped above his head, and no amount of squirming brought him closer to his goal. More lube, fingers slicking in and out, and massaging his buttocks, and again more lube. He was dimly aware of Xavier kissing his chest and sucking on his nipples, but that was merely the cherry on top of the sundae.

Xavier pulled his fingers out and moved his hand over Doran's balls and up the length of his cock. Before Doran could buck into it, the hand was gone again, but the sensory overload made him come anyway, in the most pitiful and frustrating excuse for an orgasm ever. It didn't take away his need; if anything, it honed it to a keener edge.

Xavier trailed a finger through the cum on Doran's stomach. "So impatient."

Doran wanted to strangle him, cursed him in his head, but out loud he didn't have the breath for it.

Suddenly Xavier's warmth was gone from his side, but when Doran instinctively sought it with his body, he found Xavier had merely turned onto his back.

"Whatever it is you want," he said. "You'll have to come get it."

What? No. Nonono. That wasn't the deal. The deal was . . . they didn't have a deal. "I want whatever you want," Doran panted.

Xavier hitched himself up on one elbow and skimmed his hand across Doran's neck and shoulder. His eyes flashed a careful-what-you-wish-for warning that seared like nails along Doran's spine. But what he said was, "I want you to pick your own pace for a bit."

"It's okay, really. I'm okay with your pace."

"You're in charge now."

When Doran just looked at him, trying to puzzle out the details through his buzz, Xavier shoved the pillow against the crease between mattress and headboard, leaned back on it, and tapped his thighs. "Come here."

Doran straddled him, moaning softly when their cocks touched.

Xavier ripped open a condom and pulled it on, then ran his fingertips along Doran's thighs.

Doran straightened to his knees and lowered himself onto Xavier's cock, but his breath caught in his throat at the pressure. God, he couldn't do this. "I don't want to be in charge."

"Well, if it makes you feel any better, that's not optional. This only happens if you want it and make it happen. And if you decide against it, that's fine too."

Doran closed his eyes and let his head fall back, trying to concentrate, his hands scrabbling over Xavier's legs for balance or purchase. He found his hands instead. Xavier laced their fingers together and propped Doran up. "Relax. We have all the time in the world."

Speak for yourself.

Doran tried again, ignoring the burn, chasing the amazing feeling of before, straightening up again, and going back down. He got into a rhythm that let him relax, take a bit more of Xavier's cock on each down stroke, and ride the waves of pleasure it sent through his body.

When he opened his eyes again, Xavier was still watching him, but he was breathing hard, and his brows were drawn together in concentration.

He pulled Doran's hands up to his shoulders, and Doran let himself fall forward into a kiss that turned up the heat even more. He could feel Xavier's groan as well as hear it, and his own. His body seemed to lose its form, exist in nothing but nerve points that tumbled end over end in the surf of pleasure pounding through it, mixing with his heartbeat and the harsh rhythm of his breathing. He thought he could go on like this forever, but then Xavier pulled his knees up, and Doran's cock rocked against his hard stomach, once, twice, before the world exploded against the inside of his skull and the echoes ricocheted down to his toes. He felt Xavier's thrust, felt Xavier's muscles contract underneath him, and a sudden exhale of air against his lips. Xavier's fingers, his whole body relaxed; he rolled them both over to the side, and let go of Doran's hand to secure the condom as he pulled out. All Doran could do was lie there, his head on Xavier's arm, and listen to his heartbeat.

Cool air dried the sweat on his skin and made him shiver. The mattress moved when Xavier got up and tugged the blankets over Doran, but he was too wrung out to even open his eyes. He was drifting off to sleep when Xavier came back and gathered him close, stroked his back and murmured into his hair. Something about a new moon in the hills. It sounded like poetry.

"Hmm?"

"Nothing. Go back to sleep." Then, after a while, there was another line Doran didn't catch. Was *sprightly* a word?

He fell asleep like that, with the murmur of Xavier's voice in his ear and the lush weight of perfect bliss in his limbs.

It was still dark outside when he woke up, in the dim light of the bedside lamp, a little sore, but perfectly content and snug against Xavier's body.

Xavier's fingers brushed against his cheekbone. "How're you feeling?"

"My bones have disappeared, but I've never felt better in my life." He turned his face into Xavier's palm and kissed it, unexpectedly overwhelmed by gratitude.

Xavier half turned and reached for something on the nightstand, then pressed a glass into Doran's hand. "Here. Drink."

"What is it?"

"Just water."

It took the water hitting his tongue for him to realize how thirsty he was. He didn't stop until the glass was empty. "Good."

Xavier winked at him. "Most amazing water you've ever had?"

"Something like that." He lay back, hoping he could just drift back off to sleep, but his stomach gave a long, low rumble.

"Let me guess," Xavier said. "Despite having devoured a gigantic pizza only two hours ago, you're starving."

"Sorry."

"Uh-huh. Let me see what I can scrounge up." He brushed the hair out of Doran's eyes, then rolled out of bed and went to the little fridge. "I hope sandwiches are okay, because, if you want breakfast in the morning, there's not much else here."

"Sure."

Xavier set out bread, cheese, lettuce, and mayo, and they made their sandwiches and chewed in silence.

Doran was glad of it. His brain hadn't engaged again yet, was still stumbling around somewhere in the echoes of that *"Strip"* and the way Xavier had looked him over as if Doran belonged only to him. He could get lost in that memory and in wishing he could always be that desired and confident. And, oh my god, it had been so hot.

Xavier got up to clear the dishes, and Doran scrambled to help. The little plastic clip that closed up the bread bag had turned into a complicated puzzle, as had the screw-on lid for the mayonnaise jar. That or his fingers had ceased to be connected to his brain somehow.

He was still fighting the latter when Xavier turned and took both of Doran's hands in his. Warm and gentle, despite the hard calluses that had felt so incredible on Doran's skin earlier.

"Feeling a little more yourself again?"

"Yes," Doran breathed. It wasn't a lie, though it wasn't the whole truth either. With Xavier he'd never be his old self again, and he didn't want to be. He—

"Did you get a chance to complete your sheet?"

Sheet? What sheet? Oh, that sheet. "Yeah, all ready for the next step." Tuesday seemed such a long way off.

"Show me?"

Wait. What? "Y-you want to see it?"

"I'd like to, yes."

No! Nonono. That had been an exercise for himself only. Dr. Jenkins had said so. He'd dug deep, like he was supposed to, had thought about all the garbage he'd put himself and others through, and written it down. All the crap about the lost money, and Lionel Turner and his goon, and skimming, and jail. If Xavier read all that, his face would change, and he would get rid of Doran as fast as he could. This, all of this, would be over.

"You can't make me," Doran blurted.

The light in Xavier's eyes went out. "That's debatable, but moot, because I don't want to 'make' you. I'd hoped . . ." Xavier raised Doran's hands and kissed his knuckles without breaking eye contact. "What happened that is so terrible that you can't tell me?"

Impossible to look away. *Please, please, please don't ask me that.*
Impossible to tell the truth. "Nothing."

The disappointment on Xavier's face felt like a physical blow.
Doran almost doubled over. And just like that, he was the old Doran
again, as confused and unwanted and scared as he'd always been.

He ripped his hands loose and turned his back. "It's none of your
business. I don't owe you an explanation." He didn't want to keep
secrets, but he just couldn't. Not now. Not yet.

The silence behind him stretched and bled around him like spilled
ink, until he thought he'd drown in it.

"Get dressed," Xavier said. There was no censure in his voice, no
color at all.

"Huh?" He'd forgotten he was naked.

"You heard me." Still flat.

"Why?" *No, don't answer that. I don't want to hear it.*

"I'm taking you home."

"No." It wasn't fair. He'd had a glimpse of paradise, and now it
all came crashing down around his ears. "You have no right . . . You
can't . . ." But even through his desperate anger he had to acknowledge
that this was Xavier's house, that he had every right to kick him out.
It was just so flipping unfair. "You're just like all the other assholes."
Throwing that in Xavier's face didn't make him feel better. He wasn't
even sure which *others* he was talking about, but he couldn't stop
himself.

Xavier crossed his arms in front of his chest. "You can get dressed,
or I can throw you into the truck bare-assed." He could have been cast
from bronze for all the chance Doran had of swaying him.

"Dick move." But he was too mixed up in his own head to do
more than pull his clothes back on, and he didn't put up a fight when
Xavier steered him out to the truck by his shoulder.

Tuesday's rain was doing an extended drum solo on the roof of
the bus and making the windows so blurry that Doran could hardly
make out where they were. Somewhere halfway to Port Angeles by his
watch.

At least the string of t-storms that had battered the coast all day Monday had blown through without anything worse than a couple of ultra-short blackouts, and some branches and debris in the roads. He'd called Elena, and she'd told him to hole up and stay safe, and that she'd see him next week. Doran hadn't even tried to make it into work. He'd wanted to finish some sketches of the town and to capture the lake that Xavier had taken him to, but neither worked. The one thing that had always saved him from being swallowed by a black hole failed him now, because the only thing that came out of his pen was Xavier. His face, his hands, his ass and long legs, his smile, until Doran was ready to throw his pad across the room. The more he thought about Saturday night, the more miserable he felt. And the more pissed. And he couldn't even begin to get it all sorted.

He hadn't heard from Xavier since he'd dropped him off at his apartment Saturday night. Hadn't even seen him at the gas station on Sunday, even though he'd been on the lookout for the white Silverado all day.

A tiny part of him refused to believe that he'd screwed things up beyond saving, but it was getting smaller and smaller. There wasn't really any way back, because that would involve telling Xavier that he was a thief and a convicted criminal. Xavier was gone either way, but at least this way Doran wouldn't feel like crawling in the gutter next time they met.

He couldn't even say that Xavier hadn't given him any warnings. *No secrets, no lies*: those had been his clear rules from the beginning. And hadn't clear rules been what Doran had craved so much? What was wrong with him? Did he trust Xavier or not?

He banged his head against the bus window, and an elderly lady threw him a scared look from across the aisle. He tried to give her a reassuring smile.

He'd so hoped Xavier would call. Chew him out, maybe, tell him to get his shit together, but let him know that all wasn't lost. The fact that he hadn't even shown up for his usual Sunday stop at the Gas'n'Sip terrified Doran more than he cared to admit.

The lights of Port Angeles swam into view. Doran pulled his hood up as the bus turned into the stop and got out. It was raining steadily rather than hard, but by the time he made it to the meeting, his pants were soaked, and the water had seeped into his sneakers. Great. Grand entrance of the drowned rat. All in keeping with how his week had started.

T.J. came running up the street just when he opened the door to the lobby. She smiled as she shook out her umbrella. "Miserable, isn't it? I can't wait for summer."

Doran shrugged. He wasn't in the mood for small talk. Her smile wavered. He was almost too miserable to care. Almost. "Warm wouldn't hurt." He held the door open for her, and her smile reappeared. Right. Better stop behaving like an asshole. He wasn't angry with her, just with fate in general. And Xavier. And himself.

They took the elevator up and joined the others as Kelly got ready to start the meeting. Doran listened with half a brain to him talk about wish fulfillment, motivation, and what made people do the things they did. The other half of his brain was busy daydreaming about Xavier barging in the door and bodily hauling him out of the meeting.

T.J. started talking about having gone back to her cost–benefit sheet and realizing her first assessment had been too superficial. "It wasn't really about keeping up with friends or info per se," she said. "I think it's much more about feeling connected when I'm lonely." Everyone nodded and there was a brief pause. Doran had noticed that before, how they waited a bit after one of them had said something, giving each other the opportunity to talk. There was respect in that wait, completely free of any pressure.

He found himself nodding as he listened to T.J., and it seemed natural to continue the thought when she looked at him expectantly. "Feeling connected has something to do with it for me too," he said. "I don't think I've quite figured out what I really get out of it. I have bits and pieces." He hesitated. "There's also this feeling of time and the world just falling away. Things that bug me not mattering anymore. And the thrill. Not when you place your bet, but that split second, just before the reveal, that races across your spine like nothing else in the world."

As he said it, he realized that Xavier had blown that out of the water with one kiss.

But the thought disappeared again when Karen said softly, "Right before the big letdown?"

Doran nodded. "Yeah, there's that." Damn Xavier to hell. "It makes me so angry all the time," he blurted out. He realized they had no clue what he was talking about. He hardly knew himself. But once started, he couldn't stop. He waved his hand at the backpack between his feet and the flipping sheet inside. "How am I supposed to take responsibility when everyone constantly tells me what to do and what I'm not allowed?" He didn't expect an answer and didn't get one. This was what he should have said to Xavier on Saturday, but hadn't been able to get out.

He nibbled on the skin at the side of his fingernail, staring into space. Xavier hadn't let him down, though. That shoe was on the other foot. But he had pushed too hard. "Dunno. It's all jumbled up in my head. I'm still working on puzzling it out."

Was Xavier right? Was he merely trying to replace one thrill with another? Even if he was, he didn't see what was so wrong with that. If it didn't hurt anyone? But it *wasn't* just that. He felt right, and at peace, and amazing with Xavier, who knew so much better what Doran needed than he did himself.

Xavier watching over him, taking care of him, allowed Doran to stop looking over his shoulder and to enter a zone of calm, like the eye of a storm. For the first time in his life he'd felt perfectly safe and protected. Xavier couldn't just take that away again. It wasn't fair.

Take some responsibility. Well, he was saving dimes he couldn't really spare to eventually pay his uncle back. That had to count for something, right? Right?

Fff . . . He didn't want any flipping responsibility. He was sick and tired of being responsible for every little shit that happened. *Fuck Xavier.* Oh god, he wished. Or rather the other way around.

Why hadn't he called?

Maybe he had tried to call after Doran had locked up. He could be leaving a message right now.

The rest of the meeting passed like so much background noise, and by the time Doran sat on the bus back home he'd convinced himself that in the morning there'd be a message waiting for him in the office. If, that was, he managed not to jerk off. Thinking about Xavier always made his pants tight, and the need to be touched shivered through his thighs. But he was sure Xavier would want him to endure the sweet agony until he could take care of it himself. Crap, vicious spiral of horny.

The next morning Doran started on the office messages before even putting on the coffee. As always, he noted names and numbers and sometimes questions for Jace to look into and call back whenever she'd come in, feeling a delicious sense of expectation at first, then impatience, then growing unease. When he came to the end of the messages, he stared at the phone, refusing to process the implication. Then he went back to the beginning and listened to them all again, waiting for the familiar soft *Hey*. He'd missed it, that was all.

Again. And again. Finally he just sat there, staring into space. In the back of his mind there had been no doubt that if only he could talk to Xavier, he could make things right. If he told all and asked for forgiveness, Xavier would wrap him up in his jacket and make him promise to never do it again.

Well, it looked like he wasn't about to get the chance. And really, who was he kidding? What would he even have said? *So, uh, I lost money to a card shark who then threatened to break my legs because I couldn't pay him? I was practically forced to screw my uncle's clients over, not my fault, didn't have a choice, really.* Yeah, that would go over well with Mr. Take-some-responsibility Wagner. *Oh, did I mention my aunt and uncle were the ones who picked me off the street and gave me a job? You can see they clearly deserved to be screwed over.*

He rubbed both hands across his face. Why couldn't Xavier just have been happy with what they'd had? Granted Doran didn't see what he got out of it, but surely it couldn't be about Doran telling him everything that ever happened in his life. Seriously, if he got off on forbidding Doran to come in his pants, Doran was fine with that. Just don't pretend it was about some nebulous concept of fancy higher values, when it was really all about kinky sex.

Call his limits. Yeah, right. As long as it involved being tied up. Not wanting to show certain sheets or reveal flipping *personal* information apparently didn't count.

He shoved a pile of brochures off his desk to stress the point and to feed his anger, but it didn't work. Because it hadn't been all about kinky sex. It would have been easier if it had. That would have been so much easier to replace than what Xavier had offered him. It didn't matter that he didn't have a name for it; he had felt it. Filling him out from the inside. Now there was just that empty feeling again that he was so used to, that wasn't quite pain, but that could still steal your breath away just the same.

Hot tears pricked against his eyes, and he knelt quickly to pick up the mess he'd made on the floor. If only the other mess was as easy to clean up. If only he could go back in time and tell his teenage self what he knew now, maybe he wouldn't have tried to fill the vacuum with poker. Maybe he wouldn't have lost that stupid five grand to Lionel Asshole Turner.

He sorted whale tours and cruises into one stack, studio tours in the next, then the 7 Cedars flyer and casino tours *(show and dinner included)*, and the city tours *With Shooting Locations!!! (studio entry extra)*. He took them all over to what Jace had dubbed the Take-One Wall and sorted them into their respective slots.

Blacklight Bingo? *Good lord.* He flipped the 7 Cedars flyer open. *Poker is back! Wed, Thu, Fri.* He quickly closed it again and shoved it into the wall as if he'd burned himself. He stared at the stylized totem logo as if it were going to jump him. Underneath were pictures of slot machines, a blackjack table, and a roulette wheel.

Spade had told him there was a way to win at roulette if you played a lot of rounds. But then, Spade loaded dice and had introduced him to Lionel Turner.

He picked up the flyer again and opened it. He'd never been inside a casino. There was one in Bluewater Bay, but apart from trying to stay away from temptation, being recognized by the locals and screwing up his program was not on his immediate list of fuckups to commit.

He'd always thought they were super posh places that you needed a suit to get into like in a Bond movie. But the dining room looked pretty ordinary self-serve/buffet style. And the people in the picture wore T-shirts.

Complimentary shuttle bus from Port Angeles, seven days a week. He wiped his hands on his jeans, because the flyer was sticking to his fingers. When had he picked that back up? He crumpled the sticky flyer into a tiny ball and pitched it into his trash basket.

He'd only promised Xavier not to buy lottery tickets anymore. Not that Xavier seemed to care much one way or another. Nor anyone else for that matter. Or, at least, Doran wouldn't blame his uncle if he washed his hands of him. He and Aunt Patty had done more than their share in helping him. They didn't owe him anything. On the contrary.

Which reminded him . . . He fished a dollar out of his back pocket and dug the little plastic sleeve out of his backpack that had once held traveler's checks. It was the only thing he'd taken with him from his uncle's office. A reminder of what he owed. He used it to collect the payback money for his uncle. It was getting thick; he should change some of the ones into tens at the next opportunity.

He upended the sleeve to count the notes. Fifty-two. In three and a half months he had saved fifty-two dollars. Only 3,948 more to go. Madness. Nothing he was doing made any sort of sense. What good was an effort that would never get him anywhere? He might as well take the fifty bucks to that roulette table in the casino.

Xavier— No, screw Xavier. He'd wanted so badly for there to be something more between them than just sex. Still did. But that was wishful thinking. He was on his own. Always had been, in a way.

Take the fifty bucks and multiply them. Or bust. It wasn't like his uncle knew they were there. Doran would be surprised if he even expected to be paid back. So it didn't make any difference one way or another. Nothing he did made any difference. Why not at least enjoy the ride, then?

He checked the times for the shuttle bus, settled down to work until three, then grabbed his stuff and locked up. He bought a sandwich on his way to the stop and ate it on the bus to Port Angeles.

The shuttle was one of those sixteen-seat minibuses, white, with the casino's logo on it. A group of old biddies was already waiting in front of the Goodwill that was the pick-up point. It was about a fifty-minute ride, with another stop in Port Angeles and two more in

Sequim. More old biddies. There were still a couple of seats left, but then the season hadn't started yet. They probably had more passengers during the summer, when the whole peninsula would be crawling with tourists.

The casino itself was a lodge-style building, lots of wood and totem poles. The group of ladies split, some of them following the bingo signs, some aiming for the casino itself. The noise of the slot machines was audible before he'd even made it into the foyer. Doran had to give up his backpack and hoodie at the coat check and pay a dollar for the privilege.

He walked through the tiled foyer and bought chips for his fifty dollars, avoiding the cashier's eyes as he flattened out his one and five dollar bills. A bar, a gift shop, and a self-serve restaurant lined the other walls, and a slot floor and entrances to two rather more stylish restaurants were visible through an entryway on the left.

He turned right, where the slot machines shared the floor with the card and roulette tables. It was busy, but not packed. The tables occupied their own area. Traffic here was much lighter than around the slot machines, and some tables were covered up. For a while, Doran just walked around, taking in the sounds, the lights, the carpeted floors and upholstered chairs, the smell, somewhere between plastic and air freshener, a bit like a new car.

A stage and seating area in a separate room to his left were being prepped for some upcoming show. He did the full round of the floor, then walked over to the roulette table to watch the routine.

He'd only played online before and wanted to make sure the rules were the same here before placing his bet. Only four people were playing, and bets lay between ten and fifty dollars. None of the players bet on singles. One was going for splits and corners. The other three played outside bets, which was what Doran was planning on doing as well.

After the round was finished, he sat down at the table and placed ten bucks on odds. It seemed fitting somehow. He *was* odd, in who he was and what he wanted. On impulse, he piled the rest of his chips on top of the ten and watched the wheel turn.

He expected the familiar thrill after placing the bet, was waiting for it to raise the hairs on his arms and start the butterflies in his stomach, but all he felt skittering up his spine was fear.

He was going to lose his stake and go home empty-handed. Every decision not to buy lottery tickets, every cheap food choice he'd made over the last three and a half months to save up the sorry little pile of five plastic chips was going to be for nothing.

Suddenly all of that did make a difference. That he'd tried, and that he'd now given up trying. The sandwich he'd eaten earlier sat like lead in his stomach. If it hadn't been for the "No more bets" announcement, he would have snatched his chips back off the table. His brain felt like the wheel, thoughts spinning in a dizzy circle, and then like that little ball in front of him jumping from one slot to the next.

Technically his promise to Xavier might only have been about lottery tickets, but he knew damn well Xavier wouldn't want him to sit here watching the antics of a little white ball. And not because he didn't respect Doran's limits, but because Doran had clammed up and stomped his foot like a brat instead of making his point like an adult. And because Xavier had cared too much not to push. Hadn't he? Would he have understood if Doran had tried to explain? Well, it was a moot point now. He'd screwed up. Again.

The ball came to a stop on the 33. The man next to Doran cursed softly; the guy on the other side did a fist pump. The dealer raked the losing bets off the table, then paid out the wins. Doran's little stack of chips doubled. He'd won.

When he made no move to bet again, his neighbor said something about best not to break a winning streak. Doran barely heard him. He'd chased the idea of losing around in his head so hard that it took some time for his thoughts to calm down. And when they did, when it finally sank in that he'd won, he didn't care.

He wouldn't bet again. Whatever had made him do it in the first place was gone. He didn't feel it anymore. The *Advantages of gambling* side of his evaluation sheet was empty in his mind.

He picked up his chips and went to cash them in. The place looked different than before. As if a veil had been pulled away. The carpet had stains from spilled drinks, and old holes from dropped cigarettes that the small pattern was supposed to hide but couldn't. The coins in plastic cups, the psychedelic lights and frenzied sounds of the machines all seemed more like the Puyallup Fair than a Bond movie. Fake and cheap, a sad replacement for whatever he'd come here for. What he'd been chasing all these years, really. But then, before he met Xavier, he hadn't known it existed. Hadn't even known what it was he'd been looking for.

What Xavier had offered him, that was the real thing. This? Just didn't compare.

Well, too late now. He'd lost that—no, thrown it away. The thought was like a noose around his throat, which now threatened to fill with tears as he swallowed. He blinked and stared back at the table where someone else had already taken his spot.

As he picked his way toward the foyer, his gaze caught a face in the crowd in a classic double take. Before his brain had come up with a name, his body had already dropped to one knee behind the row of slot machines.

Lionel Turner. The man he still owed over a hundred bucks to, and who wanted another thousand in interest. The man who'd threatened to break his legs and hands and face if he didn't pay.

Doran fiddled with his shoelace, trying to convince himself that he'd been wrong, that his subconscious had come up with the man's face because of his surroundings. Card tables, gambling . . .

But this place couldn't be more different from the motel room in which Turner had held his private poker tournaments. In there, it had been dim and stuffy. And Turner, pulling out a chair for Doran with his alligator smile, had been more intimidating than his stoic bodyguard by the door. Even Spade had treated the man with uncharacteristic respect.

Doran moved across the room behind what cover the machines provided, then risked a peek around the corner. Shit. Definitely Turner.

He quickly drew back behind the machine. He was pretty sure he'd ducked before he'd been spotted. But if Turner was here, wouldn't Mick, or whatever his name was, be around as well? The thought made the skin across his shoulders tighten. He half turned, but there was no one behind him he knew.

He forced himself to check past the slot machine again to make sure Turner wasn't looking in his direction, then walked across the floor to the entrance area. *Don't run. Whatever you do, don't run.*

Glad that the casino was half-empty and he didn't have to wait in line at the cash-out window, he shoved his chips across, then quickly pocketed the five twenties the cashier gave him.

His palms were sweaty as he fished the coat check stub out of his pocket. Not a lot of cover here. Only the gift shop, and that was at the other end. If Turner happened to walk around the corner into the entrance area, there was no way he would miss Doran.

Drumming his fingers on the counter, Doran barely managed not to hiss at the attendant who was searching for his stuff to hurry up. The guy was checking his ticket against every single number. Like, didn't they have a system? *Come. On.*

He could see his backpack from where he was standing, but didn't dare to call out to the guy. His voice probably wouldn't carry over the din of electronic bells and jingles, but better not to take the chance.

Shifting his weight from one leg to the other, he kept checking back and forth between the entrance to the slot floor and the guy behind the cloakroom counter. Finally the man found the number he was looking for, clipped Doran's chit to the matching half, and fumbled his hoodie off the hanger. It took him another precious couple of seconds to realize that the backpack went with it. Doran wanted to bash his head against the rack. He all but snatched his belongings out of the guy's hands, saw him open his eyes wide in offended surprise. *Eff you.*

He hightailed it outside. The shuttle bus pick-up point was right next to the entrance, too close for comfort. Doran checked his watch. Not even six thirty yet. The next shuttle wouldn't go back until seven. He was so screwed.

He decided to hide out in the trees beyond the parking lot. There weren't that many people around, but even if there had been more, he wasn't sure if it would have fazed Turner. Spade had said that Turner never let a debt go because if he did, word would get out, and everyone would start to think they could get away with not paying.

No, Doran would rather drown himself in Sequim Bay on the other side of the 101 than let himself be caught by Turner. Why, why the hell had he come here? Stupid. So flipping stupid.

He shivered in his hoodie and dug the rain cover out of his backpack for protection against the wind, and because it was wet under the trees. He pulled the strings of the hood close around his face against some early mosquitoes and shoved his hands into his pockets. He felt like Kenny from South Park. Shit. Bad comparison if there ever was one.

The ground squelched under his shoes like a wet sponge, and his feet were soaked in no time. The money he'd just won burned a hole in his pocket, and not in a good way.

He didn't want it, but he couldn't really afford to give it away either; he was too broke for that. His uncle certainly wouldn't want it. Not roulette winnings. Sordid money. Just like the sordid little piece of shit who'd won it.

A handful of people were waiting at the shuttle stop now. Two of the ladies Doran had come in with, and two guys and a woman he'd never seen before. He craned his neck to get a glimpse of the highway and almost missed the bus's white roof coming into view.

A couple left the casino and walked across the parking lot to their car. Behind them, a guy stepped outside and lit a cigarette, leaning his shoulders against the wall. Shit, shit, shit. The square jaw and hooded eyes had haunted Doran in his dreams. Mick, Turner's bodyguard.

He might have won at the roulette table, but this was so not his lucky day. He inched his way toward the edge of the trees as the shuttle made its way into the parking lot, so the minibus would be between him and the entrance. Then he waited until all but one of the passengers had made their way on, and sprinted across the lot. He turned his back toward the building as he skidded around the hood of the minibus and vaulted inside practically under the bodyguard's nose. He had to dig deep for what he hoped looked like a smile to the surprised driver, and slid low into one of the seats facing the parking lot and the highway beyond.

His heart beat so high up in his throat that he felt like he could chew on it. He half expected the goon to come and drag him off the bus, half hoped with everything he had that he hadn't been recognized. Time ticked by heartbeat by heartbeat, until the driver closed the doors and rolled toward the exit.

When Doran risked a glance back at the building, there was no one in sight. He breathed a sigh of relief and leaned back in his seat, closing his eyes.

It was fully dark and quite cold by the time the shuttle pulled up in front of the Port Angeles Goodwill, but at least it wasn't raining. Doran got off with the two ladies from that afternoon and hunched his shoulders against the wind. He was lucky, though: the bus to Joyce and Bluewater Bay pulled in on the other end of the parking lot just as he was crossing it. He jogged the last couple of yards and waved to the driver, who was nice enough to wait.

He dropped his fare into the box and slumped in a seat by the window, as tired as if he'd been working hard all day. The parking lot lay deserted now that the stores were closed, except for a rusty pickup that had been there in the afternoon, and a sleek black sedan slowly circling the lot. The way it moved made Doran's skin crawl, but it was too dark to recognize anyone inside, or even the make of the car.

He was getting paranoid. There was no way Turner could have followed the shuttle out here, was there? Had Mick recognized him at the casino? Or had Turner, and sent his man out to wait until he showed up again? Both possible, but not likely. Right? Still, he was glad when the bus pulled out and left the dark sedan behind.

When he got out in Bluewater Bay, he checked both ends of the street for dark cars, but didn't see any. The one pair of headlights he saw turned left before it reached the stop. It was the end of the line for the number ten bus, and a couple of guys had gotten off with him, making him feel reasonably safe. Not enough to stop the pricking between his shoulder blades, but enough to keep him from flat out running.

Jace was at her desk when he arrived at the office the next morning. He barely managed to mumble a "Hi," before hitting the coffee machine. He hadn't slept well, his dreams haunted by men in suits and sleek black cars. He'd never needed Xavier's jacket around him more than right now, but he knew he didn't deserve it. What resentment he'd had left about being abandoned had faded fast under some starkly honest scrutiny in the wee hours of the morning.

He was a wimp and an asshole. Xavier was right. He didn't have his life together. And he couldn't expect anyone else to pick up the pieces of what he'd broken.

He carried his coffee back to his desk, and Jace came over as he sat down.

"Something's weird," she said. "You always check the phone messages and list my callbacks, right?"

He sat up straighter, suddenly awake. "Yeees?"

Jace held up her hands. "Hey, I'm not saying you didn't. Just, I've had a couple of angry calls this morning from people who say they called before, but who're not on my list. So, just checking if something happened."

"I wasn't here Monday because of the storm, but we don't get enough messages in one day to fill our inbox. Not even in one week. Not this time of the year."

"'Kay. Just checking."

Doran thought back to Tuesday morning. "There was a power outage on Monday. I had to reset the time on the phones. But those messages come from an external service, so I don't see how that could have had anything to do with it. Unless . . ."

He looked at Jace, and she finished the sentence. "The service was out too."

Doran reached for his phone. "I'll call Uplink."

"Thanks." She went back to her desk, and Doran scrolled through his contacts and called the service.

"Uplink Communications, please hold for service or press one for callback."

Listening to elevator music and staring into space was about as much of a challenge as his brain could handle that morning, so he waited. Even "Rhinestone Cowboy" was preferable to thinking about the crap his life had become. It was even appropriate, somehow, though he didn't know where the cowboy found his optimism.

He finally got someone on the line and asked if they could be missing some messages. His heartbeat stumbled just asking the question.

"Oh my God, I'm so sorry." Her voice had a breathless quality that made her sound like an eight-year-old. "We lost some messages in a power outage on Monday and are still comparing our backups. But if you'll let me have your customer number, I can check for you."

He gave her the number, and hung out with someone "Laughing in the Rain" and a bit of Stevie Wonder until she came back.

"I am so sorry," she said again. "You do have a few messages in the backup that were lost in Monday's queue. I can send them to you as an MP3 file if you'd like?"

He cleared his throat. "Yeah, that would be great."

"I have your email on file. Again, please accept our apologies."

He assured her they were a great service, and most companies wouldn't even have bothered with a backup, then disconnected and dug his earphones out. No way was he going to listen to that MP3 over the speakers with Jace barely eight feet away. He didn't know what would be worse: that there wouldn't be a message from Xavier, or that there would be, when Doran had broken every promise with his visit to the casino yesterday.

He grabbed a pen and his notepad and opened his inbox. The email from Uplink Communications with the MP3 attachment was already there. Impressive speed. They must really be scrambling to get their stuff back on track.

He started listening to the messages, wrote down the name and number of a guy asking for callback, then the number of a woman who wanted to be sent a hotel guide but hadn't left her address.

Then, "Hey."

Doran's pen tore a hole in the paper. No name. Just that single syllable. Xavier knew it was Doran who took the messages, knew Doran would recognize his voice.

After a brief pause Xavier's voice continued, "I made a mistake. I'd like to apologize." Another pause in which Doran stared at his screen with a frown so tight it screwed up his vision.

"Call me. Please? I understand if you don't, though. I promise I won't call again." He gave a cell phone number before hanging up.

Doran completely missed the last message in the file. There was a lump in his throat the size of Mount Washington, and he wanted to bawl and throw up at the same time.

A mistake? Apologize? Xavier was apologizing. To him.

He replayed the messages, just to hear his voice again. Shivers under the skin. And the pit of despair. He'd called. But Doran had given up on him. Had gone gambling. With his uncle's money.

He needed air.

He wrote down the last message for Jace, then tore the sheet from his notepad and gave it to her. "I'll go pick up the mail."

She was on the phone, and just gave him the thumbs up. They were pretty much calling their own hours as long as they were still closed during the week, so she probably couldn't care less whether he'd even be back today.

He grabbed his stuff and escaped into the raw March morning. It had been cold ever since the storm. More like winter than spring.

Xavier's low *"Hey"* kept pinging around inside his skull. He finally had a phone number to call Xavier whenever he wanted. Only he couldn't anymore. He'd piled the ultimate screwup on top of the stuff he'd already not told Xavier. How was he supposed to talk to him after that?

He shivered in the cold air and pulled his rain jacket over the hoodie for more protection against the wind, then crossed the road to the post office parking lot and stopped dead.

White Silverado at ten o'clock. Xavier was in the post office.

He couldn't move. The need to go see him, and the need to run as far and as fast as he could balanced out in a stalemate that nailed him to the spot.

When he peered in the truck window, a bag of trail mix had replaced the power bars. No books on the passenger seat this time, but a ring binder with the Washington Department of Fish & Wildlife logo on the front.

Standing here like this reminded him of the first time he'd talked to Xavier, and he almost expected the warmth of a big body at his back. Could a guy be that lucky twice? He looked around the parking lot.

A black BMW was entering at walking speed from the other end.

Doran's heart jumped into his throat. *Black sedan.* The reflection on the windshield obscured his view.

There was no way he could reach any of the buildings without being seen. He tried the passenger door of the Silverado, but it was locked. Keeping the truck between him and the sedan, he inched toward the back. The tailgate was locked as well, but the rear window of the camper shell popped open easily.

Luckily the truck had corner and bumper steps. Doran boosted himself up, snagging his hoodie on the lock for a precious couple of seconds, then he was through. He'd be bruised from snaking his way over the tailgate into the truck bed, but at least behind the tinted windows he was out of sight. He closed the rear window and hunkered down. He'd lost track of the BMW, then saw it again when its door opened and the driver got out.

Mick. A soft moan escaped Doran.

Mick opened the rear door for Turner, and together they started walking toward the Silverado. *Shit, shit, shit.* They must have seen him when he'd gotten stuck on the tailgate. And he was well and truly trapped now. They didn't even need to hurry.

Then they suddenly stopped and half turned toward each other, as if they'd lost interest.

Doran jumped as something bumped into the truck. He swiveled around at the sound of the driver's door being opened. Xavier. The truck dipped as he got into his seat.

The dizzy relief.

Doran didn't know what kind of view Xavier had of the back, but now was a lousy time for any sort of discovery and discussion, so he silently scooted close to the cab to be out of sight as much as possible. There wasn't much room between two large water containers, gas and oil canisters, a cooler, snowshoes, two large plastic boxes, and a hiker's backpack with sleeping bag, camping mat, and what looked like a rolled-up tent or shelter. That thing must weigh a ton. A dark-green nylon bag wedged between the backpack and the boxes looked like a rifle cover.

He was freezing.

CHAPTER EIGHT

X avier flipped through his mail. More trash than content, as usual. The post office seemed to know. They had provided a large paper recycling bin by the door into which Xavier pitched his spam mail before heading into the cold. The sky had that looming oak-plank color that meant snow. Which matched the forecast of a light dusting.

Almost ten. He was running late, which wasn't the post office's fault, but the WDFW's. They insisted on way too many paper forms.

He'd have to move it if he wanted to check the Wolf Creek Trail today and then make Lillian Shelter by daylight. Weather permitting, he expected to be out on his survey round for a week. He'd been wanting to do that anyway, but now he actually needed it. Clear his head and get away from people, from anything that reminded him of the fact that Doran hadn't returned his call. From having to look at himself in the mirror while shaving.

He couldn't remember ever having gotten anything quite so wrong. That day at the lottery place hadn't been about Doran wanting to be chased. He'd just needed to know that it mattered. That he mattered. So, maybe he'd wanted to be stopped. Or maybe he'd needed to make that promise to stop to someone he mattered to.

But that day was nothing compared to how thoroughly Xavier had fucked up Saturday night. Dick move indeed. He could have whipped himself for kicking the kid out. He'd been disappointed, yes, and irritated because he'd had no idea how to make Doran comply with his program. And not for one second had he entertained the thought that maybe that wasn't his responsibility. Or even his right.

He'd been trying to help, yes, but the road to hell and all that. There was no excuse. None. No wonder the boy wanted nothing more to do with him. He wanted nothing more to do with himself.

Two guys in suits were lost in conversation in the middle of the parking lot. Probably movie people. They certainly seemed out of place enough for it.

He unlocked the car and threw the mail on the passenger seat. Nothing in there that couldn't wait until he got back.

A brief feeling of unease made him check the rearview mirrors as he slid into the seat. Nothing. Huh.

Traffic was relatively light when he peeled out of the parking lot and headed toward Port Angeles. Not as light as before the Hollywood invasion. He'd never get completely used to that. But at least it wasn't as bad as tourist season. He snorted at himself and his get-off-my-lawn grumblings. *Getting old, are we?*

He caught himself checking the mirrors again for no good reason, then turned the radio on to drown out his thoughts, and to get rid of . . . whatever ghosted across his neck. A snowflake careened off the windshield, then a second one. Good thing he'd packed warm clothes and the sleeping bag. There would definitely be snow on the ridge. Not a lot, though, with the kind of winter they'd had and the earlier melt. Probably down to mud on the trail. Well, he had his snowshoes. And he'd checked in with the WIC, just in case he got stuck somewhere.

He left the last of the cars behind as he turned down Hurricane Ridge Road, breathing a sigh of relief when the trees closed around him on either side. He didn't mind the endless mileage of the switchbacks. All that mattered was that he was alone on the road.

The chasing clouds threw moving shadows against the ground. They were thickening fast, but for now the sun still reflected off old snow. The parking lot at the Hurricane Ridge Visitor Center was just as deserted. The snow was his friend. Who needed July, anyway?

He clicked his sunglasses out of the holder and slipped them on against the glare, then continued on to the trailhead a few hundred yards down the road, but slowed out of habit as he passed the lodge, giving the building and surrounding area a quick visual check to confirm everything was okay. The road and lot were completely cleared and dry this year. The visitor center would open for business on the weekend.

Just before he rounded the bend, he saw a black BMW in the rearview mirror, one he thought he'd seen on the road from Port Angeles already. That type of car didn't usually spell winter camper. He watched it slow down and pull into one of the parking spots by the building. Probably just up here for the view and a quick picture stop. If they'd planned on lunch, they'd be disappointed. It was still off-season.

He continued to follow the road. With a bit of luck he'd be able to park in the small clearing right at the trailhead.

But when he got there, the bank was piled hip-high with snow from the plow, no room for the truck. He'd try the parking spaces farther down, then. With the way the road bent, he'd be able to cut across an expanse of open brushland back to the trail.

The parking there was indeed cleared, an SUV with California plates the lone occupant, its rear window full of destination stickers. Off-season midweek hikers had become a tad less rare with the movie crowd in town, but not by much.

Xavier pulled up next to the SUV and killed the engine; the cold air tingled on his face when he got out. There was some snow on the trail, but not enough this year to tempt any skiers down the long slope to Whiskey Bend. He took a deep breath, enjoying the view of the Elwha Valley, and let his mind settle into what he thought of as its trail rhythm. Tuned to and alert on different levels of consciousness than town and people and traffic demanded.

Walking around to the back, he pulled the woolen hat out of his jacket pocket and put it on. The air against his face was only a degree or two above freezing. At least there was no wind, and even a bit of weak sunshine still peeked through between the gathering clouds now and then.

He opened the back and was already swinging the backpack onto his shoulders when, with a kick of adrenaline, he noticed the sneakers and jeans-clad legs.

Doran, knees drawn up, wide-eyed, shivering in the unheated back of the truck. Surprise hit him so hard in the chest that he almost stumbled back. Relief, and the need to pull Doran close and warm him against his body, were quickly followed by worry and the first tendrils of anger at being jerked around, clueless, and too dumbfounded to think straight.

"What the hell?" he muttered under his breath.

"P-please, don't be mad."

Xavier couldn't decide if Doran was merely nervous or if his teeth were chattering with the cold. "What are you doing here?"

Doran obviously took that as encouragement, because he scooted forward and got out of the truck, looking around.

"We're in the park. Hurricane Ridge," Xavier offered. He couldn't seem to get his brain in gear.

"Oh." Doran was more fidgety than usual, hardly listening, more searching over his shoulder than getting his bearings.

Xavier snapped his fingers in front of his face, which seemed to get at least some of his attention. He wanted to say, *C'mon, talk to me, kid. Please, just talk to me.* But what came out was, "I asked you a question."

"I needed to get away," Doran mumbled, with a quick glance up the road.

"From what? And why in the back of my truck? It's fucking freezing in there. Look at you."

Doran, however, was still preoccupied with the road back toward the visitor center. "Did anyone follow you?"

"What?"

"Like, was there a car behind you?"

"Who the fuck cares? I'm sure there was a truckload of cars behind me today. But, guess what? I don't make it a habit to check whether I'm being followed." The faster he figured out what Doran had gotten himself into, the better, and those disorganized babblings weren't helping. He needed to warm up.

"A black BMW?" Doran asked.

Xavier felt his eyes narrow. Maybe not that disorganized. "There was one up at the visitor center. They stayed up there, though." But he had thought he'd seen the car in Port Angeles earlier.

Doran's head snapped up, and he stepped past Xavier to look across the expanse of snow to where the road curved back, then his gaze retraced the line of asphalt to the other side. "Where does the road go from here?"

"Nowhere. This is the end of it."

Doran stared at him. "We can't go back."

What? The fuck? "Oh, yes, we can. I'm taking you home. You deserve to walk, but you're not exactly dressed for a hike in this weather. I'm sorely tempted to lock you in the truck and leave you here for the next week or so until I get back."

Doran threw him a terrified glance.

"With the fucking heat on," Xavier growled.

At which point Doran obviously decided it was an empty threat. He turned toward the trail. "Were you going down there? Where does it go?"

"Get in the damned truck."

"No, you don't understand." His hand was shaking as he combed the hair out of his eyes. "They have guns."

"What?" This was getting more ludicrous by the second.

"Your rifle," Doran pointed at the back of the truck. "Is it loaded?"

"It's not a rifle. Not the way you mean. It's a dart projector, for tranquilizers. You don't just carry those around. The dose needs to be calculated for a specific target."

Doran looked disappointed, then every bit of color drained out of his face. Xavier turned to see what he was looking at, and saw a glimmer of black metal through the trees farther back. When he turned to Doran again, the kid had started running away from the car.

God grant me patience. "Doran, stop! You'll be soaked and then frozen solid in two seconds flat."

Doran kept running, didn't even acknowledge that he'd heard the warning.

"Goddamn it," Xavier squeezed through his teeth. He grabbed an old ski jacket from one of his emergency boxes, slammed the door shut, and took off after Doran.

He'd disappeared between the trees, but his tracks were easy to follow in the snow. At least he was heading in the right direction toward the trail. Xavier didn't particularly feel like jogging after him with the pack on his back. Should have taken it off and left it in the truck. He decided to let Doran run out his panic. Hopefully he wouldn't break an ankle in the process; he seemed to be slipping and sliding with every step.

Doran had veered onto the trail as the path of least resistance when he'd come to it. He had more steam than anticipated. Xavier caught up with him about an hour later, halfway down to Whiskey Bend. An opening in the trees had let some sunshine in and melted the snow away.

Doran stood doubled over, hands on his knees, head down, trying to catch his breath. He jumped nearly out of his skin when Xavier came around the switchback, then marginally relaxed on recognizing him.

"You're leaving tracks a mile wide," Xavier called out.

Doran raised a hand as if to stop him when they were nearly level. "You can't take me back," he panted. "They'll shoot out my kneecaps."

It sounded so cliché mafia movie that Xavier laughed. But Doran's eyes were wide with what was clearly terror. However fantastic he sounded, he obviously believed what he was saying. The only way Xavier would return him to the car was slung over his shoulder. Either kicking and screaming or knocked out. He didn't relish the thought of either.

Plus, that eerie feeling of earlier was back and made the little hairs on his neck stand on end. Without meaning to, he looked over his shoulder, but didn't see anyone.

"You're making me paranoid too." He handed Doran the ski jacket. "Here. Put this on. You'll cool out fast standing still."

Even over his hoodie and raincoat, the jacket was several sizes too big, but it would keep him warm until they got back to the car.

The sound of snapping twigs, then running feet carried around the bend. Doran bolted off the trail so fast that Xavier barely kept up with him. But he only ran a few yards before hunkering down behind a tree.

Xavier went down next to him to peer under the low-hanging pine boughs back toward the trail.

A big man in a suit and black winter coat had stopped roughly where they'd been standing before. He must have heard their voices and run to catch up. "Look, whoever you are," he called out, scanning the trees. "This has nothing to do with you. We just need to have a word with Callaghan." He raised his arm to wipe the sweat off his forehead, and Xavier got a glimpse of a holster under his jacket. Shit. He was carrying a gun.

Xavier turned back to Doran, trying to get past his disbelief. "Who the hell are these guys?" he mouthed.

"I owe them money," Doran whispered. "Well, I owe one of them money. That's his bodyguard, enforcer, whatever."

"You borrowed money from people who'll bust your knees if you don't pay?"

"It wasn't like that. I lost. Can we just go on now? I promise, I'll explain everything."

Xavier stared at him, trying to come up with a plan. If these guys indeed shot first and asked questions later, they couldn't stay on a public trail, especially since he knew there were hikers or campers in the vicinity, possibly just ahead. And they couldn't go on to Whiskey Bend without warning either, for the same reason.

Doran was trying to squeeze past him, but Xavier caught his shoulder in an iron grip. "How good are you on foot?"

"I'm good. I'll manage. I swear." It sounded more like desperation than anything else, but that desperation might just be what would keep him going, despite his ridiculous sneakers.

Xavier held Doran's chin and tilted his head up, studying his eyes. "Can you stay ahead of them?"

"Yes." It was plea as much as a statement.

Xavier checked his cell phone, but he hadn't really expected to get a signal down here. He wished he'd believed Doran earlier and called law enforcement from the car. Or at least taken the damned radio with him. He'd thought he'd be right back; he sure as hell hadn't anticipated being stuck out here.

A second suit came wheezing around the bend, woolen overcoat flapping around his legs. He caught his breath for a moment before asking, "Where are they?"

"Not far, I hope," Big Guy said. "Still . . ." He pointed at his shoes. "These weren't made for running around in the snow."

"Shut up. You think my feet aren't wet? Find them."

"C'mon, boss. He has to come back to town at some point, and then we got him."

The smaller suit's voice dropped so low that Xavier could barely hear him. "No one gives me the runaround, you hear me? No one! Unless you never want to work again, go and find them." The menace in his voice was palpable. Xavier wasn't surprised to see the bigger guy cave and resume his search.

He trusted himself to find his way to Idaho Creek, even if they had to cut through the woods. From there they could go straight up Lost Cabin Mountain. He'd probably get a signal from somewhere up there. Enough to call the cops. Either they'd lose their pursuers on the way up, or, if they were persistent, he'd have to make sure to keep them running around until the cops made it to Hurricane Ridge and then lead those two goons over there. He thought briefly about sending Doran along the trail to Whiskey Bend, but if he miscalculated, and the suits split up, Doran would be worse off on his own. He wanted the boy where he could protect him if needed.

"Walk close to the trees," he said against Doran's ear. "Try to step where there's no snow or mud. If you stay on the leaf cover you'll leave less of a trail. Let's hope your thugs are lousy trackers." With that he took the lead, careful to stay out of sight and not make a noise, heading away from the trail.

They'd made it a few dozen yards before Doran stepped on a twig. The resulting crack wasn't even that loud, but it made Xavier flinch, and when he turned, Doran had frozen in his tracks as if it had been a gunshot.

"Right," Xavier murmured. "I'll make shorter strides, try to stay in my footsteps."

Doran nodded, but he was only half-listening. His attention was focused backward toward the two men now out of sight on the trail.

"Hey. Eyes on me."

Doran's head snapped around. He looked searchingly at Xavier's face.

"Let me worry about who's behind us. You just concentrate on staying with me. We'll be going uphill in a while. Say something if you find yourself falling behind. I can't keep my eyes on you when I'm leading. And I don't want to turn around and find you gone. Got it?"

Again Doran nodded. "Got it." This time Xavier was sure he'd been heard.

They fell silent after that. As long as they were on level ground, Xavier kept up a distance-eating lope, and even if Doran hadn't been too scared to make a sound, he probably didn't have enough breath to walk and talk at the same time.

Xavier kept to as straight a line as he could, calculating that it would bring him to Idaho Creek at roughly the three-thousand-feet line. They'd still have a pretty steep hike up from there, but doable.

He kept checking back occasionally, but didn't see any trace of pursuit until almost an hour later, when they were starting to climb. From the mountain side he had a brief view of the two suits trying to cross the creek.

He ducked back down. So, at least one of them was a reasonably good tracker. And they didn't look like they were going to give up anytime soon.

Xavier had expected Doran to lag by now, but he'd stayed on his heels as if he'd been glued there. Nevertheless Xavier had slowed the pace when they started to climb. Doran, by his own admission, was no hiker, and Xavier carried about forty-five pounds on his back. He had to hope that the two guys were hampered by their footwear, and by having to find and follow tracks. He started to change direction now and then, partly to make the climb less steep, partly just to keep the tracker busy.

"You still doing okay?" He wasn't whispering, but kept his voice low. Sounds carried down the mountain.

Doran nodded, but Xavier could see the exhaustion in the line of his shoulders. His hair was plastered around his face and, beneath the flush that the cold air and exertion had whipped into his cheeks, he was paler than usual.

He made Xavier want to do nothing so much as to scoop him up, but he was afraid Doran would fall apart on him if he let any of that show. "It's not far now. Just stay with me."

The light was starting to fade. He'd calculated enough time to reach Lillian Shelter by daylight, and they'd traveled much less linear distance than that to where they were now, but with hiking through the brushland, uphill, and slowing down for Doran, he could've used another hour in the day. He continued up the mountain to about fifteen minutes below the top, then stopped at a rocky outcrop beneath the trees and turned to Doran. "Stay here for a moment."

Doran who'd been setting one foot in front of the other in somewhat of a stupor for a while now, immediately threw a panicked glance over his shoulder.

"We've gained some ground on them. Don't worry. I'm not leaving you. I just want to make some tracks up there. I'll be right back."

Doran swallowed and gave him a searching look. "Okay."

"Five minutes, ten at most. Stay on the rock."

He went on up the mountainside, smudging his footprints with the toes of his boots to make it seem as if Doran was still following, his sneakers obscuring the distinctive tread of Xavier's hiking boots. When he came to a fallen tree, he stepped past it, then backward across the trunk, careful not to disturb any of the moss on it. From there he set his feet very deliberately under the pine boughs of fallen branches, on rocks, wherever he left the least visible impression in the ground. In that way, he carefully made his way back down to where Doran was waiting for him, fidgeting and biting his nails. He breathed a sigh of relief when he saw Xavier.

"Told you I'd be back. Come over here, but don't step off the rock. Okay. Now set your feet exactly where mine go." In that way he led Doran around the mountain a few hundred feet below the top, hoping that in the gathering darkness his false tracks would throw their pursuers off enough that they wouldn't stumble on his camp in the night. He kept going until Doran said, "I can hardly see your feet anymore."

"It's okay," Xavier said under his breath. "That means they can't see our tracks anymore either. We need a bit of level ground, or at least— Ah, that'll do."

He wanted to pitch the tent because, with the sun down, the temperature was dropping fast below the freezing point. While the spot he was looking at couldn't be called level, it was slightly less sloped, and he thought he could wedge the tent in between the triangle of trees there, so that at least they wouldn't start to skid down the slope in the middle of the night.

He slid the pack off his shoulders and undid the straps, very glad that he knew his gear inside out, because he could barely see his own hands, and he'd rather not use the flashlight if he could at all help it. He listened for any sounds that didn't belong as he worked. It would be a tight squeeze. The little pop-up tent was one person only, and Xavier wasn't exactly small, but it would keep them dry and out of the wind.

He pulled out a couple of granola bars and touched Doran's hand with one, let go when he took it. "Eat this."

"I'm not hungry."

"Eat it anyway. It'll give your body something to burn." He opened the other one, folded it in half, and shoved it in his mouth, chewing while he worked.

As he was feeling around for straps and supports in the dark, Xavier was keenly aware of Doran next to him shifting his weight from one foot to the other. Nervous or cold, possibly both. His teeth were chattering when he asked, "Wh-what are you doing?"

"Setting up camp."

"You want to spend the night here?"

"We *are* spending the night here."

"We can't. They're going to find us in the middle of the night."

"They'll find us more easily if you don't keep your voice down. Or better yet, shut up." He was doing his best to clear the ground of any sharp objects without pitching himself down the slope in the process.

"There's not even room for the tent."

Xavier moved a few rocks aside, careful not to roll them down the slope and make a racket.

"I'm not staying here," Doran said, more quietly this time, but still belligerent as hell.

Xavier looked up and turned, even though he couldn't see him in the dark. "Excuse me?"

"I'm not." The repetition sounded less sure.

He needed to get Doran inside the tent and warm as fast as possible. He didn't have time for a tantrum. "You're welcome to leave." By now Xavier couldn't even see his hands anymore. The kid was panicky, but he wasn't stupid. He would stay exactly where he was.

"Maybe I will." But he didn't move; there was only the sound of his breathing through chattering teeth. Then, as if he was testing the idea, "Maybe I should."

"When I stumble across your body in the morning, I'll be sure to inform the authorities. Any next of kin?"

Silence. Even the teeth chatter stopped.

"That's what I thought. Shut up, Doran. You're not dying on my shift."

Xavier felt around the trunks for low branches, trying to determine the best angle for the tent.

After a minute or so Doran said, "I'm not going to make it on my own, am I?"

His voice sounded so small that Xavier gave in for a moment to his need to be gentle with him. "Doran, I know this park like I know the inside of my pocket, and I don't think I'd make it down the mountain on a moonless night like this without breaking my neck."

"I didn't mean to drag you into this," Doran said. Then, barely more than a whisper, "I just didn't know where else to go."

Xavier half turned and almost slipped, caught his hand around a branch just in time. What he wanted was to wrap Doran in his arms, but if he didn't focus right now, he'd get them both killed. "Well, I'm glad to know I'm good for something."

Finally he managed to wedge the pop-up tent between the trees to his satisfaction. It wouldn't be the most comfortable bivouac ever, but it would keep them dry.

"I d-didn't mean it like that," Doran said behind him.

Xavier opened the zipper and threw the sleeping bag and mat roll inside. He would have liked to hoist the pack up into the tree, but he couldn't see worth shit anymore. "I know." He knelt to spread the mat and shake it out and unzip the sleeping bag, then stood back up. "Give me your hand."

Once he felt Doran's hand in his, he said, "Okay, I've got you. Come here."

It was pitch-black by now, and on the uneven ground Doran lurched against him. He was shivering violently. Xavier ran his hands along his legs; he was wet to his thighs and ice cold. *Damn.* "Strip down to your underwear and give me your pants and socks. We can use the jackets as blankets.

"It's f-f-freezing."

"For fuck's sake," Xavier hissed through shut teeth, concern cutting deeper than the anger earlier. "Will you stop arguing with me and do as you're told. Strip and get in the fucking tent." He clamped his teeth shut again. Damn the boy for making him lose his temper.

But Doran finally piped down, and after a moment handed Xavier his soaked jeans and socks and crawled into the tent.

Xavier wrung the clothes out in the dark, then rummaged around for a towel and rolled them up tight in it. They wouldn't be dry in the morning, but the towel would at least draw some of the moisture out. He took his own shoes and socks off, setting them just inside the tent with Doran's sneakers and the towel roll, then shrugged out of his jacket and spread it out inside the tent. Shit, it *was* cold. He peeled off his pants and spread them out as well, wet bottoms on top of the towel, then crawled backward into the tent, trying not to knee Doran in the process.

It was a tight squeeze indeed. He managed to snake under the sleeping bag and pulled Doran close against his body. No argument there, at least. Doran pressed up against him as if he was going to claw his way under Xavier's skin. Well, in a way he already had, hadn't he? *Fuck.*

He needed to keep some sort of distance to be able to concentrate on getting them both out of this alive. Wrapping Doran up in his arms, trying to stop his shivering and warm up his icy feet and legs, didn't make that any easier.

He redistributed the jackets for best coverage and clamped Doran's hands under his armpits to warm up his fingers.

Doran buried his face against Xavier's neck. "I wish I could always be like this," he murmured.

"Freezing your ass off?"

A weak chuckle. "No, just close to you."

Xavier swallowed hard. The urge to claim Doran as his, body and soul, was overwhelming. "Why didn't you call me back?" His voice rasped in his throat, and he hated his need to ask.

"Didn't know you'd called," Doran mumbled. "Storm took out the power, backups only came in this morning, and by then . . ." He trailed off, and Xavier was about to prompt him to go on, when he said, "When I'm with you, I feel like nothing can ever hurt me again."

Xavier had to fight the urge to swear that nothing ever would. He couldn't promise that. But he could damned well try. He slowly ran his hand up Doran's neck and threaded his fingers into his hair. He didn't think the resulting shiver had anything to do with the cold, was suddenly very aware of their groins touching through nothing but underwear, and the fact that neither of them was unaffected by the close proximity of their bodies.

He wished, not for the first time, he could sweep all the mess-ups and miscommunications down the mountain. There was so much he wanted to say, to ask. He wanted to know Doran inside out, and wanted Doran to know him.

But Doran was beat, even though he'd held up a hell of a lot better than Xavier had expected. If he didn't sleep now, Xavier would never get him moving again in the morning. And he was still unsure where they both stood. There were some questions left that he needed answers to.

Doran trusted him enough to come to him in an emergency, but he was far from forthcoming with his past, and Xavier was too aware that kicking him out hadn't helped any trust issues at all.

Well, he could keep trying, couldn't he. "Sleep. You'll need your strength."

CHAPTER NINE

When Xavier had stopped to pitch the tent, Doran had been sure he'd be asleep on his feet in seconds. But now that he was actually as cozy as it was going to get, he couldn't doze off, even though he was totally shot. How Xavier had kept that punishing pace with the huge pack on his back he had no idea.

He closed his eyes, trying not to listen into the night, trying to get lost in the big, warm body he was so deliciously wrapped up in, but too conscious of how pissed Xavier had to be at him, and with reason, to truly relax.

Plus, he hurt everywhere, especially his feet, especially now that they were thawing out. And despite all that he was half-hard and too aware of knees brushing thighs, and solid muscle under his cheek. He flinched when Xavier shifted his feet against a particularly sore spot on his heel.

"Are you hurt?"

"Just a blister."

But Xavier was already hitched up on one elbow, fishing for something in the backpack. How he found anything in there in the dark was a mystery. He dove under the sleeping bag and got a hold of Doran's ankle. Light from a flashlight briefly spilled out at Doran's throat.

"Christ." Xavier came back up, rummaged in the backpack some more and dove back under the cover with his flashlight. Doran found his foot seized again, something cool on the back of his raw heel, then light pressure. Band-Aid probably. Xavier checked the other foot and turned the flashlight off before he resurfaced. "You'll have to walk again tomorrow."

"Sorry." The concern in Xavier's voice brought a sudden wave of shame, and exhaustion got the better of him. He had to blink the tears out of his eyes. "God, Xavier, I'm so sorry for everything."

"Sorry doesn't sweeten my tea," Xavier grumbled, but he cradled Doran's head against his throat again and pulled his body tight. Doran deeply breathed in the scent of his skin.

It was cold, the ground under the sleeping mat was hard and bumpy, and they both needed a shower. He still wouldn't have traded his place for anything in the world. He was pretty sure that part of his mushiness was just because he was so exhausted he could have cried himself to sleep. But there was also some weird magic going on here. Pizza dinners and kisses in bus stops might have fed his crush, but running from guns in the melting snow, and Xavier's grumbling concern, was turning it into something else entirely. He wanted so badly to give something back, but he didn't have anything Xavier would want.

"Why didn't you say something?" Xavier asked against his hair.

"You have other things on your mind," Doran mumbled, half-embarrassed, half-happy about Xavier fussing over him.

Xavier's hands on both sides of his face, thumbs caressing his cheekbones, forehead touching his. "*You* are on my mind. When am I going to get that through your thick skull?"

Doran could barely swallow around the lump in his throat anymore.

Xavier fell quiet for a moment, then continued, "I'm not asking you to trust me. But I'm asking you to trust that I know what I'm doing. Out here, I mean. In the park."

"But I do trust you. You said I trusted you too much, remember?"

A breath like a laugh in the dark. Or maybe annoyance. Doran couldn't tell.

"You trust me with your body, but you have more secrets than a confession box. I can't help you if I don't know what's going on."

Doran wasn't stupid enough not to realize that Xavier was busy saving his ass because he himself hadn't taken care of his own shit. "This is not about the blister anymore, is it?"

Xavier was quiet for so long that Doran thought he wouldn't answer, but then he said, "I've told you from the get-go that secrets are a deal breaker."

He had. Doran caught himself wishing for a second that Xavier could just be content with not knowing. But then, of course, he wouldn't be Xavier. The kind of guy who wanted to face his problems so he could then go and solve them. Not like Doran, who much preferred sticking his head in the sand, hoping that they would somehow go away.

After a pause Xavier added very softly, "But I shouldn't have ridden roughshod over you and demanded your trust the way I did. Especially after reading you the riot act about trust needing to be earned. I was way out of line, and I apologize unreservedly for that."

Doran shook his head. He wanted to say that Xavier had been right, that he had nothing to apologize for, but no sound came out. Because what would he follow that up with? He could barely see why Xavier was putting up with him now. If Doran told him everything he'd done and not done, there'd be nothing left but contempt.

But he couldn't let Xavier think it was his fault either. "It's not about not trusting you. Maybe, in a way, it's about not trusting me. You know? I don't see the attraction, I guess. What makes you put up with my shit. I dunno. Why'd you want to put up with even more shit?" In a way it was easier to talk into the dark, but still hard to find the right words. "You're so . . ." Well, *straight* didn't quite cut it. Doran felt a grin tug at the corners of his mouth, despite everything. "Clean," he finally said, because that was the only word he could think of that came close. "And I'm such a crummy mess."

Xavier took a deep breath, but didn't say anything. Instead his hands tilted Doran's head back just a little, and then Doran felt lips on his own. Soft, just brushing across, the feather touch running like a current through Doran's body, as if Xavier had thrown a switch. Air came rushing out when he opened his lips in response. Xavier's gentle nips and licks turned his insides to Jell-O, growing more insistent until Doran's lips tingled, until the edge of who he was melted into Xavier and there was no doubt left in the world about who was in control here. Held firm and spinning dizzy at the same time, he heard the moan leave his throat as if it came from far away. The only reason he still knew he had legs was because the heat finally flooded into his frozen toes.

"'Each kiss a heart-quake,'" Xavier murmured against his lips, and Doran couldn't have agreed more. He was trying to catch his breath and wanting to drown in Xavier's kisses at the same time.

"Since I can't seem to convince you otherwise how much I want you," Xavier said, "that'll have to do. And if you still think that came from indifference, I'm afraid I can't help you."

Weird magic indeed. No way in hell could Doran explain it, but he was starting to believe it.

"I am not going to leave you," Xavier said.

And that, too, Doran started to believe. The tears he'd been holding back seeped out from under his closed eyelids, and he didn't care. Xavier brushed the first one away with his thumb, then pulled Doran close again, so the rest soaked into the shoulder of his sweater.

He became aware of Xavier's heartbeat at the side of the neck, Xavier's hands stroking his hair and his back. Then Xavier's voice. "Tell me?" Not a command. A request and an invitation. With a gentleness that made Doran's throat tight all over again.

And suddenly it all came spilling out, about Spade taking him to the "real" poker games, and how cool he'd felt to be "in," to be one of the players. To belong. Of Turner letting him play on, even after he'd run out of money. The rush, the losing track of it all.

"I was so stupid," he whispered. "When I came out of it, I owed him five grand. More money than I've ever seen in one heap in my life. I tried to get a loan . . . Like I said, stupid beyond belief."

The scams he'd pulled at the office to pay Turner back, ten and fifty bucks at a time. "I convinced myself that taking little bits from people who didn't even notice wouldn't be so bad. I know it's a lousy excuse." He took a deep breath, Xavier's shoulder a solid pressure against his cheek. "I tried to get Turner to give me more time on the last hundred or so I owed him. That's when he told me that there was still the small matter of interest. Another thousand."

"Why didn't you go to the cops?"

"To tell them I owed money for illegal gambling? And what if Turner found out? You didn't see his smile. Or Mick slapping a baseball bat into his hand. That shit makes one sick sound."

Xavier's hand on his back stilled and tightened a little.

And Doran plowed on. How his uncle had caught him just before he'd made it, and had reimbursed all the customers out of his own pocket. How one of them had filed charges anyway.

"When they locked me up, before the trial, I couldn't even think about being sorry or anything. I was scared shitless someone in there would find out I'm gay." He tried a laugh. "Like that would have made a difference. But I was lucky. My uncle bailed me out. Can you believe that? After everything? And since it was only a C-class felony theft and my first offense and all that, they let me out on probation, some community service and mandatory therapy."

Xavier didn't say anything, just ran his hand through Doran's hair, and Doran found himself talking of things he'd never told anyone before: his mother and her church, the Homosexuals Anonymous crap he'd walked out of, how she'd kicked him into the street then, and how his uncle had taken him in. "He's the last person in the world who should have had to pay for me."

"Are you in touch with your uncle?"

"Yeah, I send them a card or a letter a few times a month, just to let them know I'm okay."

He fell silent, hoping against hope he wouldn't hear the disgust in Xavier's voice. He didn't want to have to remember that too. The way Xavier's face had looked when Doran had disappointed him last weekend had already burned itself into Doran's memory.

"Thank you," Xavier said softly.

Huh? "Thank you?"

"For telling me. That can't have been easy."

"You're not fed up with me?"

Xavier's voice was rough when he said, "Oh God, kid. I'm not saying you didn't make some bunk decisions, but only after everyone whose responsibility it was to protect you, your parents, your church, your friends, pulled every conceivable rug out from under your feet."

Doran could hardly believe his luck. So tempting to just leave it at that. But if he didn't keep going now, he'd never be able to again. And it felt good too, not to have to hold on to all that rot. More than anything he wanted to let it all go and not have to check himself every time he talked to Xavier. No secrets. He crossed his fingers and toes.

"I went to the casino on Wednesday. In the shuttle bus. It wasn't anything planned. It ... just sort of happened." He bit his lip, waiting for Xavier's comment. When it didn't come, he went on, "After promising you. I tried to tell myself the promise was only about lottery tickets, but I knew it was a cop-out. And that's where I ran into Turner."

Xavier continued to thread his fingers through Doran's hair.

"I have no idea what I was thinking. Well, I wasn't, really. I didn't mean to make you angry, I swear."

"I have no right to be angry with you." He didn't sound angry. Just quiet. Disappointed?

"You have every right. I led them straight to you."

"You needed help. I'm glad you came to me. Even after I let you down. I told you to call your limit, and when you did, I wasn't listening."

"I ... I might not have been explaining it very well."

"No, I was being a self-righteous ass. I was so busy making sure you would keep up your end that I dropped mine. That was entirely my fault."

"You did try to call me."

"Yeah, well, you didn't know that."

It was like he was dreaming. A dream where everything suddenly went right for no reason. He couldn't believe Xavier understood. He didn't deserve this. Any of it. And there wasn't even anything he could do or say to repay him. Or was there?

"I think I'm done with it. The gambling." Would Xavier even care? Although he'd cared enough to be ticked off about the lottery thing.

"That's good." It sounded more carefully neutral than convinced.

"You don't believe me." Not that surprising, really. People said things like that all the time, didn't they? Was he just saying it? "Can't say I blame you. But when I was at the casino, even before I saw Turner, it suddenly seemed so fake. Like, I won, but it didn't mean anything. You know? Like figuring out a magic trick. Once you see behind the illusion, it's boring, it doesn't work anymore."

Especially after getting a taste of some real magic. But he didn't say that. There'd been enough mushiness for one day. Plus he didn't want Xavier to think he was just replacing one addiction with another.

Because he wouldn't cave again at the next hitch, the next fight, the next time things got rough, right? Right? A tiny quake in the pit of his stomach shook the dead certainty of before. He knew he'd been sucked into a lie, but would he remember? "I really want to be done," he added more quietly.

"I believe you."

And just like that he could breathe again. He snuggled deeper into Xavier's shoulder, his limbs grew heavy, and he drifted off.

He wasn't sure what woke him up, but Xavier's body next to his was all tense muscle, and just as he was about to ask whether there'd been a real scream, or he'd been dreaming, Xavier clamped a hand over Doran's mouth and whispered, "Shhh," against his ear. Doran's heart leaped into his throat. He tried to catch a sound, anything outside the tent, but there was only silence and pitch-darkness.

He had no idea how long they'd stayed frozen like that, when Xavier's muscles relaxed, and the hand brushed across his face and hair.

"Did someone scream?" he whispered.

"Could have been an animal," Xavier said under his breath.

"You think so?"

After a brief pause Xavier said, "Not really."

No secrets, no lies. It went both ways, and was weirdly more reassuring than if Xavier had tried to give him false comfort.

"It didn't sound too close," Xavier said. "I'll check it out as soon as I can see something." He shook his head. "City slickers. Crawling around on the mountain in the dark."

"They'll never give up," Doran whispered, but in his secure fortress of one, the thought was less scary than it had been before.

Xavier snorted. "At this point they're probably more lost than anything else. Try to go back to sleep."

He woke to the sound of the tent zipper as Xavier disentangled himself from the sleeping bag and crawled outside. It wasn't light yet, but the darkness was less thick, outlines faintly visible in the gray.

"Time's it?"

"Dawn. Sun will come up soon." Xavier pulled his pants on and stepped into his boots, squatting to lace them up. "I'm going up top to try and notify the WIC and the cops, then have a look around. See if I can find out what happened last night." He stuck his head back in and grabbed his jacket. "Stay in here and keep warm. It's freezing. There's fresh powder on the trees."

Doran rubbed the sleep out of his eyes, trying to get his head clear. A bird was starting to chirp not far away. "Wouldn't it be safer to wait for the cops and have them look around?"

"Maybe. But whatever I might wish for in my more uncharitable moments, I can't just ignore a potential emergency, or sit here and wait for someone else to do my job. It doesn't take long to freeze to death up here without shelter and if you can't move."

A million scenarios flitted through Doran's mind, each more terrifying than the one before. Some of that might have shown on his face, because Xavier bent down to kiss him and said, "I'll be careful. I promise."

It felt normal and took him by surprise at the same time.

Xavier left him a handful of granola bars and a thermos, then shouldered the backpack and disappeared from Doran's field of vision.

For a minute Doran stared at the half-open zipper of the tent flap. It was getting lighter by the minute now. He scrambled out of the tent to . . . he didn't even know what. Catch another glimpse? *Sucker.* But Xavier had already disappeared between the trees and moved so quietly, despite the weight on his back, that Doran didn't even hear him anymore. All he heard was the rising chorus of bird song.

There was a dusting of snow on everything, icy under his bare feet, the cold air raising goose bumps on his legs. He crawled back under the sleeping bag and took the towel roll with his pants and socks with him to warm them up a bit. They were still damp and felt like he'd just taken them out of the fridge. Great.

After a while he unrolled the little pack, thinking they might actually warm up faster if he put them on. It was uncomfortable but not too bad. It felt like forever since Xavier had left, but when he checked his watch it was only seven. Couldn't have been more than an hour, then, could it? When did it start to get light? He'd never paid attention.

The thermos held apple juice. He drank some and ate two of the granola bars, trying to make them last. It passed the time, and he didn't know when Xavier would be back.

When the sun came up and hit the tent, he grabbed the ski jacket Xavier had given him and wrapped himself up in it before crawling outside again. The snow on the top of the trees was already melting under the sun, little droplets sparkling like diamonds in the light. Pretty. He stretched his arms above his head, then touched his toes, or tried to. He wished he had his sketch pad or something else to take his mind off the fact that there were two armed assholes on this stupid mountain and Xavier out there trying to find them.

Unless that scream had come from someone else entirely. What were the chances? From what Doran had seen of off-season tourist traffic, not high. A lot of the roads in the park were normally closed this time of year. And despite the mild winter, some of them still were.

He shivered, and it wasn't only because of the cold. He felt exposed and helpless on the mountainside, expecting all the little sounds the forest made to turn into movement between the trees any second. But to stay inside the tent, where he couldn't even see if anyone was coming, was worse. The ground sloped quite a bit, and he started up in Xavier's footprints as far as he could still see the tent, which wasn't far. The tracks in the snow were already melting, so he didn't dare go any farther. He'd probably get his ass lost on top of everything else if he did. Besides, Xavier had told him to stay put. He intended to do just that.

He found a couple of rocks he could use as a sort of exercise stepper. Just when he was getting into a reasonable rhythm, a shot rang out.

He froze, one foot in midair, arms out for balance, and listened. Nothing except the blood pounding in his ears, and his brain screaming Xavier's name.

Then a second shot.

This time he thought he'd gotten the direction it had come from. A little below and to the left, somewhere around where they'd come up the day before.

He started running toward it, trying to stop the flood of images in his head, all involving Xavier and blood. Skidding on the wet, snowy ground, stumbling over branches and unseen stones, tearing the skin of his hands on trees and rocks, trying to keep his balance. He pulled the sleeves of the jacket over them for protection and tried to keep going in a straight line. The slope of the mountain and the slanted sunlight helped him keep his bearings.

Breathing got more difficult, the cold air burning in his throat and making him cough. He slowed down, both to catch his breath, and because he didn't want to accidentally run into whoever had fired those shots. He strained his ears, but any sounds had stopped with the gunfire. The trees around him were quiet; nature holding its scared breath. It raised the little hairs on his neck.

Then the sound of something crashing through underbrush and soft swearing, ahead and above Doran. He pressed himself against the trunk of a tree, throwing the occasional peek toward where the sound had come from. He couldn't see anything, but heard the snap of a twig, a little lower down this time. Definitely someone moving through the trees just ahead. And definitely not Xavier, by the voice.

He moved a little to the side, around some bush with leftover black berries and dropped flat when he caught movement out of the corner of his eyes. Dark suit, dark hair. Mick, the bodyguard. His back was turned toward Doran, his attention focused on something on the other side of a larger clearing.

The snow was melting underneath Doran and seeping into his pants. He couldn't stay here. As quietly as he could, he got up on his knees and scooted over to a large, moss-covered rock sticking out of the ground. From here he could see partly into the clearing, which looked like it had been made by some sort of landslide. Tree stumps and rocks covered nearly level ground in front of a rocky outcrop. Xavier's backpack leaned against the rock wall, next to someone rolled up in one of those silver foil emergency sheets.

It trapped Doran's breath in his chest; little bright spots started dancing in the air above the rock. He squeezed his eyes shut. *Pull yourself together.* It couldn't be Xavier. If he'd been shot and could still move, he wouldn't roll himself in a blanket in plain sight. Doran risked another glance. Mick was walking away from him, along the edge of the clearing, looking intently at a fallen tree on the other side.

When Doran squinted between two low hanging branches, he could just make out a shoe and part of a leg behind the tree trunk. Dark-green pants, hiking boots. Xavier. Trapped. And the guy with the gun edging around toward him. *Shit. Shit. Shit.* How did you take out someone with a gun if you were unarmed? All he could do was throw rocks at the guy.

Which . . . might not be the worst option. He was close enough for a good pitch.

Taking care to stay covered, he started hunting around for some throwing rocks. He found two fist-sized ones and one slightly smaller.

Weighing one of the larger rocks in his right hand, he gripped it loosely with just his fingertips for minimum friction. He wanted a fastball, and with the rough edges of the rock that would be difficult enough without gripping it tightly. He hadn't thrown a baseball for way too long, but he didn't have time to think about it too much. He rolled his shoulders, loosening up the muscles for an overhand delivery.

He'd have to step away from his cover and take Mick by surprise. Which meant he'd probably get only one chance. *Windup* as he stepped into the clearing, *pivot* toward Mick, *stride*, and *follow through*.

Gun raised, Mick had turned toward him on *stride*. The shot rang out as Doran swung around into fielding position, using his momentum to dive into the underbrush. He'd known his pitch was good as soon as he'd released the rock. His shoulder crashed into a slim tree, hard enough that it would leave a bruise. He lay still for a heartbeat, two. There were no more shots.

Turning, he risked a peek through the tangle of branches he was lying in and saw Xavier running along the outside of the clearing in a crouch toward where Mick had been standing. There was a gun in his hand. For a moment Doran wondered where it had come from. Then some of the puzzle pieces fell into place. The guy in the blanket must be Turner. Xavier had taken his gun, which meant he'd been armed this whole time and not nearly as helpless as Doran had imagined.

Doran squeezed his eyes shut. Relief at seeing Xavier unhurt was closely followed by unease. Would Xavier be angry that he hadn't listened? That he'd left the tent and come running down here after Mick, despite having been told explicitly to stay put?

He hadn't done badly making his own decision, though, had he?

He scrambled to his feet, and tried to move his shoulder. There was a bit of a twinge, but nothing that indicated anything more than a bruise.

Xavier had hunkered down where Mick had fallen, but he kept throwing glances in Doran's direction. Better go over there and face the music. Throwing that rock had seemed like the thing to do at the time, but with the adrenaline draining out of his muscles, he realized how high the chance had been that he would miss, that he'd get shot.

Xavier stood up just as Doran reached him. He'd tied Mick's hands and feet with what looked like climbing rope. "Are you okay?" He ran his hands down Doran's arms at the same time, as if to make sure.

Doran nodded. He'd apparently knocked Mick out cold, and the bodyguard was just now starting to come around. Because he'd swiveled toward Doran at the last minute, the rock had hit him square between the eyes. A trickle of blood ran across his forehead. He looked like he'd been executed.

"That was a hell of a throw," Xavier said. "You weren't kidding when you said you had a mean pitch arm."

Doran grinned, something like pride warming him from the inside out. He nodded across the clearing at the silver blanket. "That Turner?"

"Yup. It was probably his scream we heard. He must've skidded over the edge up there." Xavier indicated a break in the brush at the top of the rock wall. "And dropped the fifteen feet straight down. Completely blew his knee out and broke his wrist from what I can tell."

He was cradling his right arm as he talked, and Doran noticed a tear in the sleeve of his jacket. "You're hurt."

"I'm okay. One of the bullets got a bit too close, but it didn't even hit the muscle. I was lucky. Guess I should put something on it though. Give me a hand here?"

Together they dragged Mick over to where his boss lay. Doran's brain hadn't kicked back in yet, and his body was working mainly on autopilot. He did notice Xavier's concerned looks, though and tried to pull himself together.

There was a first aid kit open by the backpack. Looked like Mick had snuck up on Xavier while he was busy patching up his boss.

Xavier shrugged out of his jacket. There was a large bloodstain on the sleeve of his sweater, and when he pulled out of it, Doran saw a deep gash along Xavier's upper arm. It was still bleeding, but not too badly. Xavier fished a small package out of the kit and ripped it open with his teeth. A wet wipe of some sort that he used to clean the blood off his arm. He ripped open another package with a rectangular dressing with adhesive edges, like a large Band-Aid. He held it out to Doran. "Not sure I can get it on straight with one hand."

Doran winced when he pressed it on Xavier's arm, but it didn't seem to bother him.

Xavier put his sweater and jacket back on and dug one of the guns out of his pocket. "Have you ever fired one of these?"

Doran shook his head.

"I managed to get a hold of the sheriff's department. They're sending their SAR helicopter. Should be here soon enough if nothing goes wrong. I'd still like to get a fire going, just in case, and then go get the tent. This asshole—" he nodded his chin at Turner "—cooled out more than I'm comfortable with. And I'd prefer for everyone to make it out of here alive. Asshole or not."

Doran nodded. He hadn't really cared whether his rock would kill Mick when he'd thrown it, but now, thinking about it, he'd rather not have that on his conscience for the rest of his life.

"Can you keep an eye on these two while I'm gone? It won't be long. Ten, fifteen minutes."

Again, Doran nodded.

"Do you want me to leave you the gun, or would you feel better with a pile of throwing rocks?" His voice was gentle, letting Doran know that either was perfectly fine. He also sounded like he was talking someone down off a ledge.

Doran shook himself and cleared his throat. "Rocks," he said. "I'll go find some rocks. I'm good with them, and we're no worse off if I screw up and lose them." He threw a quick glance at Mick, who had his eyes closed, but Doran was sure he was listening to every word they said. Even tied up, he gave Doran the shivers. Something told him that people like Mick stopped being dangerous when they were dead, and not a second earlier.

CHAPTER TEN

Doran was a bit more quiet than Xavier would have liked, so he kept checking to see whether the kid was okay as he walked around collecting firewood. But he didn't seem hurt, which was the main thing. He was already starting to pull it together, just needed a little time. It wasn't exactly an everyday situation to find himself in, and he'd reacted well under stress. Way better than Xavier had expected, actually.

Damn, if anyone had told him about that throw, Xavier would have dismissed it as a tall tale. He still couldn't quite believe the deadly accuracy of it, or the controlled precision of Doran's movements when he'd stepped out from between the trees. Not as helpless as he sometimes looked. *Holy shit.* Definitely something to remember the next time he worried about Doran's instinct of self-preservation.

He threw another look over to where Doran had settled on one of the larger boulders with a good view of the clearing, a small pile of rocks at his feet, far enough away from Mick that he couldn't be jumped. No need to worry about him. He might have made some stupid decisions in the past, but he was no fool. The thought shed a different light on the trust Doran was extending him.

Most of the wood he found was damp, but as long as he could get the fire started, the extra smoke would just make it easier for the helicopter crew to find them. His main concern was Turner, who'd shown signs of moderate hypothermia and seemed to be in considerable pain. Not that he didn't deserve it.

Mick would be okay. Xavier had a strong suspicion he was ex-military of some kind. He had no idea how the two goons had gotten separated or why, and he didn't much care, but it seemed Mick hadn't had any problems weathering a night on the mountain.

He finally had enough wood together that he thought might burn, but had to resort to one of his WetFire cubes as a starter. The terrain was too soaked to provide even a small amount of dry tinder.

Once Xavier was satisfied the fire would burn for a while, he looked around for a reasonably level spot, cleared some rocks away, then got the little spray-paint can out of his kit, and laid out a large X for the pilot.

Doran, crouching on his boulder, watched his every move. Alert and with it now.

"Right," Xavier said, walking back over. "I'm off to get the tent. Keep an eye on Mick. Keep your distance, don't let him reel you in with talk. I'll be back before you know it." Even now it was hard not to get lost in those smoke-blue eyes.

"What about Turner?" Doran asked.

"Don't worry about him. He's had it." He allowed himself a brief touch, just a fingertip along Doran's cheekbone. "You'll be fine."

"I know." There was a confidence and determination in those words that hadn't been there before. Surprise again.

Xavier wasn't sure what was going on in Doran's head, if he was even aware of it, but he wasn't about to complain. He gave Doran the foldable shovel from his pack. "If the helicopter comes in before I'm back, bury the fire. The rotor blades have a nasty habit of kicking shit just about everywhere."

It was easy to follow Doran's tracks back to the tent. He'd been flat out running, skidding in not a few places, leaving very visible gouges in the snow and mud. Xavier ruefully shook his head. No question who had flown to whose rescue here.

All this time he'd been so careful not to physically hurt Doran that he'd been oblivious to the real danger. He'd lost his head to the temptation Doran presented to his own bullheaded temperament and trampled over his real fragility. And Doran had been ridiculously easy to strong-arm, had played right into it. Because he *had* trusted Xavier, and because he'd been desperate for any sign from Xavier that said *I care*. Even punishment.

Knowing what he knew now— He had to stop to catch his breath, so nauseous suddenly that he might have thrown up if there'd been anything in his stomach. He'd done exactly what everyone else in Doran's life had done: abandoned him. That hadn't been his plan or intention, but from Doran's point of view, that must have been what it had looked like.

He pushed himself off the tree he'd leaned against and picked his way through the underbrush to the campsite. If Doran gave him the chance, he'd do whatever he could to make it up to him. It was a big if.

Rolling up the sleeping gear and breaking down the tent took only a minute. He'd done it so many times, he'd be able to do it backwards and skunk drunk.

He heard the helicopter when he was halfway back. By the time the pilot had zeroed in on his mark and touched down, Xavier was stepping through the trees into the clearing. The fire was indeed out, Doran crouched, head down, at the foot of the wall.

Three men came over as soon as they saw Xavier's uniform. The medic, whose name tag read *Peterson*, was a stranger, but he'd met one of the deputies a number of times and gone to school with the other, Mike Young, who winked at him. "Hey, X. What're you up to this time?"

Xavier nodded a greeting, and when Mike held out his hand, awkwardly shook with his left. "Curse of wide shoulders," he apologized. "Always stick out too far."

"Can't leave you alone for five minutes, can I?"

"Apparently not." He gave them a quick rundown of events and Turner's condition as they crossed the clearing, then let them do their job and rejoined Doran.

"Ready to go back to civilization?"

"I guess." There seemed to be some fascinating aspect to the rock he was holding that utterly escaped Xavier.

"You guess? I would've thought you had about enough of freezing, blisters, and getting shot at."

Doran grinned. "Yeah." Then he looked up at Xavier with a smile that didn't know if it was welcome. "I'd like to do it again sometime, though. Without the getting-shot-at part."

Xavier was conscious of a small hitch in his breath. "Would you, now?" He shoved both hands in his pockets, hyperaware of the men going about their business by the rock wall. "The possibilities that opens are nearly endless," he said quietly, and was rewarded with Doran's eyes widening for a second before he lowered his head and studied the rock in his hand again.

Damn. He wanted to draw Doran close and kiss him breathless. He couldn't have cared less what anyone thought of him, but they'd both still have to sit through questioning, and the whole thing would go down much more smoothly if the officers didn't have to deal with their preconceptions. Being smart about it didn't mean he had to like it, though.

Doran stayed close during the short flight to the hospital, seeming to crave touch even more than Xavier did. The occasional brushing of shoulders wasn't nearly enough.

At the hospital, Xavier watched Turner being wheeled away under guard, then insisted on having Doran checked over for frostbite, even though it was unlikely he wouldn't have noticed by now. He needn't have worried. Apart from a largish bruise on his shoulder, Doran was fine.

A nurse cleaned out the bullet graze on Xavier's arm and applied a new dressing, then it was over to the sheriff's office, where Mick was booked, and Doran and Xavier gave their accounts of the morning and the day before. Doran called his office to let them know what was happening, and by the time they were done, it was afternoon.

Xavier's stomach was growling like a bear's fresh out of hibernation, and he badly wanted a coffee that didn't taste like battery acid. He went over to where Mike was signing some paperwork. "Are you guys going to send someone to retrieve Turner's car?"

"Yeah, sheriff was just talking about it. You parked up at the ridge? Want a ride?"

"That would be great. Thanks."

When he told Doran he was going to get the truck, the kid grabbed his jacket.

"There's a Safeway with a Starbucks across the road," Xavier told him. "I can pick you up there when I come back. Gives you a chance to eat something besides granola bars." Just the mention made his stomach protest loudly again.

"It can wait. I'd rather come with you. If I may. I won't say a word, I swear." He fiddled with his zipper and looked for all the world like a kicked puppy.

It reminded Xavier forcefully of his thoughts that morning. Making Doran feel abandoned again was the last thing he wanted. Maybe Doran was more badly shaken by the morning's events than he'd thought, after all. "By all means, come along then, saves me a trip."

They were quiet on the ride up, three abreast on the bench of the tow truck. Mike had started a bit of chitchat, but turned the radio on when all he got in return were monosyllables. Xavier had talked more that morning than he usually did in a month. He was all talked out. And Doran seemed lost in his own thoughts.

They found the black BMW parked next to Xavier's truck. The SUV with the travel stickers, Xavier was glad to note, was gone. He and Doran got out, and Mike started to maneuver the tow truck into position.

Xavier unlocked his truck, but paused when Doran made no move to walk around to the other side. He ran the backs of two fingers across Doran's cheek. "How're you holding up, Superpitcher?"

The quip earned him a shy smile. "I'm okay. No need to worry about me." But there was the tiniest crease between his eyebrows.

Xavier decided to give him a bit more time before calling him on the polite lie. "You better get used to someone worrying about your well-being," was all he said.

Doran threw him a grateful look, but didn't reply.

Xavier gave a short wave good-bye to Mike, then opened the door. "Let's get you back to civilization. Hop in."

Doran kept up his unusual silence, even when they were alone. Now and then he threw Xavier a quick glance.

Halfway between Hurricane Ridge and Port Angeles, Xavier decided he'd had enough time now. "Talk to me. What's eating you?"

A mumbled, "Nothing," was his reply.

This was no good. He pulled over to the side of the road and killed the engine. Ignoring Doran's startled look, he got out, walked around the hood to the passenger side, and opened the door. "Out."

Doran scrambled out of his seat and stood in the wedge of the open door, shoulders up, hands jammed into his pockets. "I'm sorry," he blurted out.

"Don't be sorry. Just answer the question."

Doran's eyes were huge, dark circles underneath speaking of not enough sleep. Xavier traced one with his thumb. "Am I pushing too much again?"

Doran shook his head. "I'm just thinking about the trial. I wish I didn't have to, you know . . . be there?" The unspoken *tell everyone why Turner was after me* was easy to hear in the pause. He leaned his face against Xavier's fingers, and Xavier brought his other hand up to cup his face.

"I'll be there if you want me," he said.

"Really?"

"You have my word."

"They are going to lock him up, right?" Doran asked after a brief silence.

"I most certainly think so."

With a deep breath, Doran finally expelled some of the nervous tension. "I'm sorry I left the tent, when you told me not to. When I heard the shot. I thought . . ."

Xavier tilted his chin up, so he could see his eyes. "You did good. You heard the shots and reacted to a changed situation. I had no idea the two of them had separated, and there was a good chance Mick would find me before I found Turner and his gun. And even though he didn't, I'm more used to a rifle than a handgun." Again he cupped Doran's face in one hand and ran his thumb along the dark hollow under his eye. "That rock of yours couldn't have come at a better time. You saved my ass back there."

Doran grinned. "I did, didn't I?"

"Now, don't get cocky," Xavier growled, but he didn't mean it, and judging by Doran's widening smile, he knew that. He tumbled against Xavier's body, snuck his arms into his jacket, and hugged him hard around the waist, his face pressed into Xavier's chest.

Xavier tried to ignore the sudden constriction of his throat, and wrapped his jacket around the narrow shoulders. "Stupid kid," he murmured against Doran's hair, and got no protest this time. Part of him didn't want to let go, but the side of the road wasn't the place. "Now, if you don't want me to pass out from starvation, you'd better get in the truck and let me take you back to Port Angeles. I know a place not far from the water where they serve a mean biscuits and gravy. To say nothing of their pie."

He felt Doran laugh against his chest, before he pulled away and looked up. "Priorities, right?"

"Right."

There was a lot more he could have said, about priorities, wants, and needs. But he didn't think he could take any more sentimentality on an empty stomach. Besides, it was starting to look like they'd have a lot of time to talk about things.

Their early dinner did a lot to make him feel more in charity with the world. The triple espresso might have had something to do with that as well. Doran's face had a bit more color too, though he'd probably sleep like the dead tonight.

He'd had to park a little further up toward the Gateway Transit Center, and as they walked back to the car, Doran slowed down in front of a stationer's window. There was the usual display of file folders, expensive pens, and desk organizers. One corner was taken up by an easel and an assortment of tubes and brushes. Xavier tried to follow Doran's gaze.

"They've had it on display for months," Doran said. "It's a completely ridiculous price for a box of pencils. Which is why they can't sell it, of course." His voice gave the lie to the contempt in his words.

The box of pencils in question was a large wooden case with a hinged lid that, when opened, revealed a two-tiered set of artist's pencils and accessories. The red sale tag read $282.95.

Doran didn't stop, but his head turned as he slowly walked past the display, until he tore his gaze away and stretched his shoulders, then shoved both hands in his pockets. "Ridiculous," he repeated.

In his mind's eye, Xavier saw him stopping in front of the window every time he was in Port Angeles, with that wistful look in his eyes, imagining the feel of the pencils in his hand, the way they'd move across the paper, knowing he wouldn't be able to afford them for a good while to come at best.

It was almost enough to make him walk into the store and buy them for Doran right then and there. He knew both the price and the joy of good tools, and the thought of what Doran would be able to do with them was hard to ignore. But while he was far from hard up, three hundred bucks wasn't exactly a box of chocolates. Doran was too conscious of his straitened circumstances not to get prickly at a gift like that. And Xavier needed to be absolutely sure the dynamics between them were free from constraint before giving a gift that could so easily be misinterpreted as racking up an obligation.

The closer they got to Bluewater Bay and Doran's apartment, the more Doran fidgeted in his seat. "Are you taking me home?" he finally asked, staring straight ahead at the road.

Xavier's instinct told him the last thing Doran wanted right now was to be alone. He decided to trust it. "I thought you might want to change, grab a toothbrush. That sort of thing."

The smile he got lit up Doran's face like a Christmas tree. *Jackpot.*

He waited in the car as Doran raced upstairs, then came racing right back with a plastic bag under one arm in no time. The sky was getting darker by the minute. Dusk and rain clouds rivaling with each other to cover the town first. Headlights went from nearly invisible to bright beacons.

They made a brief stop at the Tourist Information, so Doran could try to get his backpack. Luckily Jace was still there. Xavier watched from the car as she hugged Doran and talked at him with big gestures. It looked like she was pelting him with questions, which Doran quite literally ducked. From what Xavier had overheard, he'd kept it very brief on the phone, only saying that he was okay and would be back tomorrow.

"Phew," Doran said, when he'd slammed the door of the truck shut and leaned back in his seat.

"Narrow escape?"

"Kind of. I said you were waiting, and I'd tell her tomorrow." He closed his seat belt with a frustrated shove. "I have no clue what to say, though."

Xavier stayed silent as he pulled back into the road, firmly reminding himself that it wasn't his decision. He hated any kind of smoke and mirrors, but he could understand that Doran didn't want to air the details of his life in public. Who did, really?

"I'm glad," Doran said softly, "that you didn't drop me off."

"Me too."

Doran flashed him a smile. "Really?"

Xavier nearly banged his forehead against the wheel. He didn't know what to do anymore to get that across.

He wasn't aware of having allowed himself any visible reaction, but Doran quickly said, "I know. You told me that you want me."

His disbelief was so thick between them that Xavier said, "But?"

Doran squeezed his thighs, first with his knuckles, then between thumb and knuckles.

Xavier looked back at the road.

"Sometimes I can feel it," Doran said. "And then again . . ." He seemed to be struggling for words, and Xavier's fingers cramped from gripping the wheel too hard while he waited for an answer.

Finally Doran said, "If you want me, why can't you accept what I'm offering?"

What? It hadn't even occurred to him that Doran would take his caution as rejection, when all he wanted was to keep him safe. Especially after the fiasco with the evaluation sheet. He didn't know what to say, and concentrated on the turn off Highway 112 down toward Sadie Creek.

Doran hung his head.

Shit. "Because the thought that I could hurt you scares me to death," Xavier blurted out. "You never tell me to stop. Or when you do, I'm too m—"

"Because I don't want you to stop. You've never done anything I didn't want. Not even really when you asked me about the sheet. Except when you took me home, maybe." He was pale under the moving lights of oncoming cars.

"Exactly."

"But that was my fault as much as yours. I was being a brat, and you called me on it. We were both not listening." His fingers beat a quick tattoo against the dash. "Just . . . when you took me home, I thought I'd blown it. That you didn't want me anymore."

Xavier swallowed hard. "Honestly? I didn't know what else to do. My default mode in difficult situations is to retreat and regroup. I think better when I'm alone. Only, for you that was the worst possible reaction."

"You didn't know that. I have to tell you these things." He sounded so over-the-top earnest that Xavier threw him a quick look, and God help him if the little shit wasn't winking at him.

A surprised laugh escaped him. "You do."

"You'll have to keep me close." And there was that nervous tattoo again.

"Very close." That earned him a brief smile.

"Other than that, if you're really giving me the choice, I don't want you to change a single thing. Don't stop pushing."

"I can't be your parent, Doran, and, hell, I don't want to be. Nor your therapist."

"I know. I have to figure out my own shit. I get that, I do. I might need a little help now and then, though?" He started to chew on the edge of his thumb. "And to know that you . . ." He trailed off.

"That I'm here? I am. That I care? I do. Quite a bit, actually."

Again that quick sunshine-over-the-gray-lake smile. "So don't change. Please? I feel perfectly safe with you. Always have."

Yeah, because Xavier was second-guessing himself at every turn. He deliberately stretched his fingers, first one hand, then the other, trying to analyze why he was so tense.

Fuck, he knew why. Because this was important. Because he was scared to assert the power Doran gave him. Scared to take on that responsibility. And because, despite all that, he was turned on beyond belief. "Promise me you'll tell me to stop if you ever have the slightest doubt."

For a heartbeat they stared at each other, neither backing down, but then Doran, breathing hard, nodded. "I promise."

Xavier consciously relaxed his muscles. Maybe he was just looking at this wrong. His fear wasn't necessarily a bad thing. It was there to prevent mistakes, keep him on his toes. Doran's wistful trust was an extravagant gift, not to be taken lightly. He *should* be scared. He *should* be second-guessing himself. And he shouldn't let that stop him. He'd always have to question himself around Doran, and that wasn't a contradiction at all. That was simply the way it was.

He became aware that beside him Doran was watching him, awaiting his comeback with at least as much tension as Xavier had been awaiting Doran's a moment ago.

The headlights skimmed over trees on either side of the deserted track. No one but him and the Forest Service used it.

"Close your eyes."

Doran let out a relieved breath, then promptly leaned his head back and closed his eyes, a hint of a smile on his lips.

"Legs apart."

The tension in the car changed as if a switch had been flipped. Xavier grinned. *Jackpot again.*

He had to force himself to concentrate on the side of the road. The track that led down to the cabin was too easy to miss in the dark.

Out of the corner of his eye he saw Doran's hands move up and down his thighs, wanting but not quite daring to touch himself. Good.

When he pulled up in his usual spot in front of the cabin and killed the engine, he could hear Doran's harsh inhale and the ticking of the motor, nothing else. He clicked the flashlight out of its holder under the steering wheel and turned it on. Doran's eyes were still closed.

"Don't move."

Xavier got out of the truck and turned to close the door. A nervous flick of the tongue over those seductive lips. Other than that Doran didn't move a muscle, though those in his neck might be a little more rigid than before.

Damn, he was enjoying this. He went around to open Doran's door, playing the flashlight beam like a caress up his legs, over the unmistakable outline of his cock, the fingers curled into the edge of the seat on either side.

He leaned over to click Doran's seat belt open, then couldn't resist the little crunch between his eyebrows and, cupping Doran's face, placed his thumb there and smoothed it across the brow.

Doran swallowed, and his lips parted, soft, full, the lamplight playing off the blond stubble on his jaw.

"You're doing good," Xavier murmured against the corner of his mouth, barely touching, just enough to feel the tremor running through the lithe body. "Right. Out with you." He stood back, but close enough to catch a blind stumble, and led him inside. "Stand here. Don't move."

Since he'd expected to be gone for the week, he'd let the fire go out, so it wasn't exactly warm in the cabin. He quickly went about starting a fire in the stove and feeding it enough wood to keep it going for a couple of hours. Then he stood and moved Doran closer to the heat. He set the flashlight on the counter, beam up. He could turn the lights on, but he liked the shadowy, unreal light and the deep pools of darkness it conjured.

He ran a finger under Doran's jaw, watched every breath, every flutter of lashes. Slowly, he pulled the zipper of the ski jacket down, brushed the jacket off Doran's shoulder, and let it drop to the floor.

"Take your shoes off."

When Doran kicked out of his sneakers, he added, "Socks too."

Even blind and on one leg Doran kept his balance, his even movements belying his rapid breathing and flying fingers.

"Sweater."

One smooth move got rid of both the hoodie and the T-shirt underneath. Xavier let it go, feeling the impatience gnaw at his own control now.

Doran's hands hovered above the button of his jeans. Xavier pushed them aside, just to make a point of who was calling the shots, then hooked a finger in Doran's waistband and pulled him close.

Now he did lose his balance, but caught himself before Xavier's arm closed around him. Again his tongue darted out across his lower lip.

Xavier followed its path with his own, felt a rush of breath against his lips, softly caught Doran's between his teeth, then let him go again and stepped back.

"Pants."

Nothing teasing about the way Doran shed his clothes this time; he was out of his jeans with the speed of desperation.

Xavier flicked the flashlight off. "You can open your eyes if you want, but don't move."

In the darkness, Xavier closed his eyes to give his other senses a chance to take over. He ran a hand up Doran's shoulder and pulled him in again, concentrating on the pulse fluttering against his hands, the lips half opening under his skimming thumb, the quickly expelled breath, and the gulp of a new one.

He brushed his lips against Doran's, savoring their softness, their melting yield, listened to the soft, drawn-out "oooh" when their bodies touched. He was hard enough to strain his pants, but he was aware of that as if it were happening on a different plane that he didn't have to deal with right now. He focused all his attention on Doran. The way Doran curved his body into Xavier's, the goose bumps that sprang up on his skin when Xavier grazed his nails down Doran's spine.

He knew when Doran's knees would give out before he felt the weight in his arms and, the layout of the cabin as clear in his mind as if it had been daylight, he gently picked him up and laid him on top of the bed.

Neither of them had spoken for a while now, and Xavier doubted that Doran remembered how to. To be the one who could bring him to that point filled him with a heady sense of power that was so inextricably intertwined with his arousal, and a compelling protectiveness, that he couldn't even begin to imagine any of those emotions without the others. Within the cocoon of velvety darkness he could admit to himself that he *wanted* Doran to surrender and rely on him. To trust him. It was also true that he needed to trust Doran, but he needed to trust himself first. Trust himself and question himself at the same time. Like walking on the edge of a blade. Nothing had ever seemed as dangerous, and nothing had ever turned him on like this. Like Doran.

Doran. Eyes still closed, Xavier knelt on the mattress by his side, exploring his body from the tips of his toes to the roots of his hair with feather-soft wanderings of his fingers. They registered the tight muscles in his neck and arms, the fists seized into the blankets, the rapid rise and fall of the chest, the straining hips.

The sounds Doran made shortened Xavier's breath and coruscated like champagne bubbles in his blood. From soft, inarticulate moans to little cries of desperation every time Xavier's fingers wandered closer to, but didn't quite touch, Doran's cock.

He was pleading aimlessly now, syllables getting lost in his breathlessness or forgotten by a preoccupied brain.

Xavier whispered his nails up the inside of Doran's thighs and under his balls. Doran's knees jerked up, dislodging Xavier's hand. He whimpered as he lifted his ass off the mattress, but when Xavier didn't resume his touch, he flattened his legs against the blankets again, though maybe a little wider apart than before. Xavier repeated the maneuver, and this time Doran trembled in anticipation when the hand moved closer to the juncture of his legs.

He gasped when the fingers touched his balls again. "Xavier?"

"Yes?" Xavier couldn't help but smile at what he knew Doran was going to ask.

He barely got it out, he was breathing so hard. "May I come? Please?"

"You can come whenever you want, my sweet." But still he didn't touch Doran's cock. And Doran knew better than to try himself. Or maybe he had forgotten that he could. Which, *hot damn.* The whole slim body was a straining, trembling mess now. Xavier could feel him falling apart under his hands, hot skin slick with sweat. He bent over and kissed Doran. Not the gentle brushing of lips as before, but an unequivocal claim, thorough, unhurried, and absolute. And Doran gave himself up to it, wide-open with trust and need.

Without breaking the kiss, Xavier ran his fingertips up Doran's thigh again, but this time he kept going upward and laid his warm palm over Doran's cock, lightly curling his fingers around and letting them rest there.

That was all it took.

Xavier swallowed Doran's shout against his lips, licked the groans off his tongue, and curled his arm under Doran's neck, pulling him in close, not just absorbing but devouring the shocks that kept running through his slender frame, charges that exploded into Xavier's body, more ecstatic and powerful than any orgasm of his own could have been. For a heartbeat he thought he had screamed into the darkness, but all he did was cradle Doran's head under his chin and allow himself to shatter in the pounding waves of energy and raw lust Doran was unleashing in him.

When his heartbeat had slowed to something more akin to normal, he gently extricated himself and flicked on the bedside lamp. Doran's skin was cooling down fast, and Xavier got up for a warm washcloth and a towel. He cleaned Doran up, pulled the sweat-soaked blankets out from under him and draped them over a chair, then got a clean sheet and dry blankets from the closet and covered him up again.

Doran was still completely out of it. In the faint lamplight, his lashes threw exhausted shadows across his cheeks. Xavier stretched out next to him, and without opening his eyes, Doran snuggled back into the curve of his body.

With a lump in his throat, Xavier brushed the hair out of his face. He felt hollow inside, washed out. Like he imagined the come-down after some drug. It had certainly been the trip of a lifetime. And addictive. He hadn't even shaken the lassitude out of his muscles, and somewhere in a recess of his brain already lurked the question of when he could have that again.

CHAPTER ELEVEN

Doran woke warm and replete, his body all but humming with contentment. He didn't want to move, didn't even want to open his eyes. Xavier's heartbeat against his cheek, comforting and hypnotic.

In his dreams he had hoped that sex could be like this. That he wouldn't have to trade warmth and trust for the edgy excitement he craved, but that he could have both. It made him want to explore all the unspoken things Xavier still had locked away in his mind. *The things I could do to you . . .* He shivered.

"Hey, sleepyhead." The low voice not helping with that shiver. At all.

Doran opened his eyes to sunlight slanting in through the window, picking out the woolen fuzz of Xavier's sweater clear enough to make his nose itch. He rubbed a hand over his face and turned on his back to stretch the sleep out of his muscles. "Morning. Wow, I slept like the dead."

Xavier hitched himself up on one elbow. "You sure did. How're you feeling?" The sun hit his eyes, turning them luminous, like polished tourmaline, but alive, and warm, and smiling. "Doran?"

"Huh?"

"You okay?"

"Hell yeah."

Xavier's smile grew wider, and he ran a finger along Doran's cheekbone. "I'm glad." He swung his legs out of bed and got up, stoked the fire, put the kettle on, then rummaged through a cupboard.

Doran watched him, feeling like he was still asleep. No thoughts in his head, just this perfect peace.

"No eggs this morning, I'm afraid. I didn't expect to be here. We have oatmeal, though. And I think there's a can of thick cream and some canned peaches in the pantry."

He pushed up his sleeves as he reached for the coffee can, and it hit Doran that he was still fully clothed. He sat up, guilt threatening his serenity. Memories of letting Xavier pamper him, completely oblivious to what Xavier might need or want.

He jumped out of bed. "I'll get it."

Xavier looked at him over his shoulder, then faced him. "What's wrong?" He stepped in Doran's way and raised his hand to smooth out a crease between Doran's eyebrows he hadn't even been aware of.

Doran opened his mouth, then closed it again. He couldn't very well ask if Xavier had come. It was just too embarrassing. "Nothing." He tried to shrug it off and turn away, but Xavier's fingers under his chin demanded eye contact.

"When I ask you a question, I expect an answer, not a brush-off." Despite the flinty words, his face was gentle, the dark eyes concerned more than anything else. *I'm not letting this go*, they said, *because I care*. But there was something else as well, a question in the V of the eyebrows, asking if this was okay, or if he was pushing too hard.

"I just . . . I feel like I've taken advantage of you," Doran got out, trying to suppress a sudden need to pluck at Xavier's sleeve.

Xavier swept his thumb over Doran's lips, a roguish light in his eyes, and a knowing, lascivious grin curving his mouth. Like he remembered something downright wicked. But nothing like that had happened. Then he shook his head and smiled at him, and Doran lost his train of thought.

"I assure you, nothing could be further from the truth."

His brain had pretty much hung out the *vacancy* sign when Xavier had told him to close his eyes in the truck. He remembered being undressed or undressing, or a bit of both. He wasn't too sure about the details after that. He'd been quite floaty and out of it there for a while, but he was sure he'd remember if Xavier had fucked him or done anything that would even remotely explain that light in his eyes. All he remembered were teasing, light touches that had turned to agonizing bliss the longer they lasted. And the most spectacular orgasm in the universe.

"Go take your shower and get dressed," Xavier said. "I'll whip us up some breakfast."

Usually the shower woke him up, but not this morning. He was still mystified when he scrambled into his clothes. His brain refused to catch up. He'd lost his balance when Xavier had called out pieces of clothing with that growl in his voice. His whole body flushed with sudden heat at the memory. If he thought about it too long, he wouldn't be able to sit and eat.

Xavier had set out two bowls of steaming porridge, thick with cream and peaches, and a mix of sugar and cinnamon on top. He brought the coffee mugs as Doran sat down and winked at him. "Something tells me you could have used eggs today." His words and his smile seemed to have teamed up to keep Doran's skin in a permanent state of goose bumps. He'd always gotten under Doran's skin, but something was different this morning.

Whatever was between them was more intense, somehow, and felt more secure at the same time, more solid.

Doran's stomach growled, an insistent reminder to start eating already. And it was darn good too.

Every time he looked up, Xavier was studying him with that strange light in his eyes, and Doran had to look down again, because the heat would be back, and he'd be rock-hard and begging on the floor because, because . . .

He stuffed a spoonful of porridge in his mouth to silence the moan that was forcing its way up his throat. Oh god. Every nebulous wet dream of a million lonely nights had come true at once and been poured into the chair on the other side of the table. There was no way he wouldn't come in his pants even in public when Xavier looked at him like that. He was so doomed. Because . . .

His head rocked up as the realization hit him of what exactly had changed.

A slow smile spread across Xavier's face. As if he knew exactly what had just dawned on Doran.

Xavier had claimed him, made him his. Yes, he'd already promised not to leave Doran the night before in the tent. Had explained that his holding back had not been about not wanting Doran. But last night, that had been his commitment, body and soul.

The recognition of what that meant with all its implications filled him up with more bliss and happiness than he thought he could hold without exploding.

"Think you could stand spending some more nights here?" Xavier asked.

"I wish I could just move in," Doran blurted out.

One of Xavier's eyebrows went up, but the corner of his mouth twitched. "Careful. No internet."

"I don't care." He grinned. "Not much." He thought for a minute. "What about satellite?"

Xavier burst out laughing. "I'll look into it. But for now, let's get you into town, so you don't miss any more work."

Xavier was gone all week doing whatever he'd been going to do when Doran had crashed his party. He hadn't been sure when he'd get back in, but that was okay, because Doran knew now that he would be back. He threw a quick look toward the back room where he'd hung up the ski jacket Xavier had left him so he wouldn't freeze. It was warmer than anything he owned, but the best thing about it was that it was Xavier's. Something he'd worn, and that Doran could wrap himself up in. Something that would remind him, when things got difficult, that he didn't need or want to play lottery tickets or poker.

Jace had left at five to spend Saturday night with a friend. She'd said something about dinner and a movie, and Doran had stayed to finish up some ads for the website. He turned the screen off, then stretched his shoulders and stuffed the last of the pizza in his mouth. On his way to the break room he folded up the pizza carton so it would fit in the trash can, then shrugged into his/Xavier's jacket and grabbed his backpack. Lights, keys.

The sky was a stunning gradient from inky blue to bright orange, promising a sunny day tomorrow. It wasn't too cold, but Doran burrowed into the jacket regardless, luxuriating in the feel of it.

A truck slowed down next to him and kept pace. White Silverado. Conjured by the power of the jacket. Doran's heart did a happy somersault as the window rolled down and Xavier's voice said, "Get in."

He was in jeans and a black fleece jacket, and he smelled freshly showered. "Hey," he said, as Doran climbed in the truck and immediately got lost in that eye-corner-crinkling smile.

Doran tried to remember to breathe. "I missed you."

"Good."

Huh? He'd expected the usual, *Me too* or *I wasn't gone that long*. But then Xavier never did the expected, which was part of the turn-on.

"Have you eaten?" Xavier asked.

"Yeah, pizza."

Xavier laughed. "Why am I not surprised?" He turned east on Main, and Doran leaned back in his seat with a contented sigh. East meant Xavier's place. Meant walls covered in bookshelves, orange fireshine in the stove, and . . . whatever Xavier had in mind for the night. The thought made him fidget in his seat.

He was waiting for Xavier to say something, tell him to close his eyes again, or whatever, but Xavier was watching the road and the now-familiar turnoffs to less traveled roads.

He'd better stop thinking about the *whatever* or he wouldn't be able to keep it together. "I've been working on the website," he said, just to say something. "For the Tourist Information, I mean. The design of the old one was just awful. It's a virtual environment, obviously, just like the newsletter." His words ran together; suddenly he couldn't stop talking. "Doesn't need an office. Just internet. Could be done from anywhere, really. Not that I know if they'll keep me when my program runs out. Hard to believe it's been three months already. Or will be in a week. But if they did, which they might, because they said they're happy with the stuff I've done, I mean, it can be done from an office, obviously, just that it can also, if you wanted . . ." He trailed off.

"What you're trying to tell me," Xavier said, "is that if I had internet, you could work from my place."

Doran nodded. No way could he get any more words through the thing that called itself a throat.

"In fact, there wouldn't be any need for you to go back to your apartment, even?"

Why was it so hard sometimes to read Xavier's face? There was nothing but faint amusement. Or was there? Around the eyes? Doran's heart beat so hard that he was sure Xavier would be able to hear it. "Not if you wouldn't want me to," he whispered.

Xavier let the car roll to a stop in front of the cabin. "Out."

He marched Doran inside, stood him in the middle of the room and slowly turned him around. Everything neat, as always, with the typical little signs of someone living there: a mug on the drainboard, a book with a bookmark on the table, a folder and a map open by the computer. The brand-new computer. With a router. And a satellite modem.

"You have three guesses," Xavier said by his ear. "And the first two don't count."

Doran closed his eyes. He was dizzy suddenly, his throat was too tight to swallow, and under his lids the tears burned too hot. He quickly blinked them away and gulped in some air. He turned in Xavier's arms and hugged him tight, leaning his forehead against Xavier's shoulder.

For a while Xavier just held him there, then he nudged Doran's head up and winked at him. "It's pretty neat to have internet, I confess." He peeled himself out of his jacket and hung it on one of the hooks on the door.

Doran tried a grin. "Right?" It was all he could come up with. His brain, all his insides were a happy, dazed mess. He stared at Xavier, the color-obsessed part of his brain registering the orange T-shirt and how it played up the tawny warmth of Xavier's skin.

Xavier took the backpack from him, slipped the jacket off his shoulders, and hung them up too. Then he came back. Taking Doran's face in his hands, he said, "I want you as close as I can have you. Finish your program, and once you're cleared for access again, move in with me. Please?"

He sure as hell didn't have to think about that. "Yes. Oh god, yes, please."

Xavier nodded toward the computer. "Do you want me to put a lock on anything?" His voice was carefully neutral. Letting Doran decide what he wanted, what he thought he needed.

Doran stared at the dark screen, trying to push thoughts of all the arts and sports stuff he'd be able to access out of his mind, and to force himself to think about those other pages, poker, mostly. He was pretty sure he could do this. He'd been thinking a lot about this whole gambling crap this past week. His whole life, really. Past, present, and possible future.

"No. I think I'm good, and I need to know if I'm right." He shifted his weight to the other foot. Now was as good a time as any to bring it up. "I was thinking, I mean, if you're okay to drive me to the bus, just until I can afford a car again, I mean, that I'd like to stay in the SMART group for now. You know? Just until—"

"Shhhh."

"I'm babbling again, am I?"

"Just a bit." There was that smile again. The one that wiped every rational thought from his brain. Then Xavier said, very deliberately, "It's your decision whether you want to stay in the group, your battle to fight. But if you need a spot of solid ground to stand on for the battle, I can be that ground. Of course I'll drive you." Then, just before things could get too serious: "You're aware there's no pizza delivery out here?"

Doran laughed. He felt so good he could have danced. "I'm aware. I'll manage."

Xavier's expression changed then, that wicked light back in his eyes. He tilted Doran's head up and kissed him. Like he had a week ago. A kiss that said, *You're mine, and don't you forget it.* It lit Doran's skin on fire and made his heart pound in his ears.

"So," Xavier said against his lips. "I have you all alone out in the woods. I wonder what I'm going to do with that."

Doran held his breath.

"Strip."

Oh god, yes. He peeled out of his clothes as fast as he could, aware that he couldn't have denied how turned on he was if he'd wanted to.

Xavier took a scarf off one of the door hooks, and made a twirling motion with his finger.

Doran swiveled around. He felt the warmth of Xavier's body behind him. The soft wool of the scarf on his arms, his shoulders. Xavier's breath on his neck.

"Cross your wrists behind your back."

The thrill that ran through his body as he did immediate and undeniable. The scarf snaked around his wrists, tying them together, tight, but not painfully so.

Xavier went past him to one of the kitchen cabinets and came back with a tea towel he folded on the table, diagonally across and then into a narrow strip. He stepped behind Doran again, holding the towel above Doran's head, then lowering it in front of his eyes. Giving him all the opportunity in the world to protest. Or maybe Xavier knew how much it turned him on just to think about being blindfolded.

"Close your eyes." Xavier's voice, low and hoarse, sent ripples of goose bumps across Doran's naked skin as Xavier tied the towel in place.

"Feet apart. Shoulder width."

He didn't think he could come just from Xavier's voice, but he sure felt like it. Xavier was walking around him; he could feel the little brushes of warm air, then lost track of him. Seconds ticked by. He was so hard it was almost painful, and he couldn't suppress the little kitten sound coming out of his mouth. He flinched when there was the tiniest of touches on the inside of his knee. A finger? Moving up the inside of his thigh, about halfway. Then the same touch on the other leg. Then nothing. Nothing.

Xavier's body against his back and arms across his chest. Xavier's lips against his ear. "Breathe, boy. Don't forget to breathe."

He took a deep breath, and Xavier stepped away again. *Concentrate on breathing.*

A graze above his navel moving upward along his sternum. His nipples suddenly sensitive, craving touch. As if Xavier had read his thoughts, the finger veered to the side, but disappeared before connecting. A heartbeat. Two. A nail scraping across his nipple, the sensation shooting straight down to his dick. Something between a breath and shout whooshed through his throat. He felt like he was floating, the only things connecting him to the world Xavier's voice and fleeting touches. Multiplied by being unseen and unexpected.

The scarf loosened from his hands, but before he could protest, Xavier had slipped one arm around his shoulders, the other behind his knees, and was picking him up. Then the mattress, cool under his back.

"Arms up." The scarf back around his wrists, securing his arms to the bedframe above his head. His whole body so tight with need he had to concentrate again on breathing.

A shift in the mattress and the heat of Xavier's body told him he had stretched out alongside Doran. Sudden heat on his nipple, Xavier's mouth, teeth, sucking, biting. This time he did shout, and the heat disappeared.

"No, don't stop." He was surprised to hear his own voice. The answer was a quick nail flick against his other nipple, almost painful, a bolt of lust that had him arching off the bed.

Hands around his ankles, pushing his feet apart and up to his buttocks. Long, slick fingers opening him up, sending liquid fire through his veins. The contours of his body dissolving, the only sound he heard the blood rushing in his head. Xavier's weight against the back of his legs, stretching him, long strokes filling him until there was nothing left except the fiercest need to come. But he didn't even have enough body left for a voice to beg for it.

Then Xavier pushed his knees out of the way and rocked forward, his weight finally providing the pressure and friction Doran so desperately sought, his lips and tongue swallowing Doran's shouts in a hungry kiss as the darkness exploded into a thousand tiny points of light, leaving him deaf, blind, and mute, and every muscle and bone in his body turned to water.

He was dimly aware of movement, of his body being moved, wiped clean, and finally cocooned in warmth and Xavier's heartbeat.

He woke in the dark and briefly touched his face, but the blindfold was gone. It was just night.

Xavier's steady breathing at his back changed into a yawn. The small movement had been enough to wake him up. "Hey."

"Hey." His throat felt rough, as if he'd been screaming. He couldn't remember.

Xavier's arms around him tightened briefly, one hand caressing his chest. A soft kiss on his neck. "Are you okay?"

"I'm . . . How does it still get better every time?"

Xavier kissed his shoulder, his lips grazed the collarbone, then whispered across Doran's jaw. "I don't know," he murmured. "I just know that I can't get enough of you."

Words like spiked hot chocolate, warming him from the inside out.

Before he'd collected enough thoughts for a response, Xavier had rolled out of bed behind him, and flicked on the bedside lamp.

Doran turned to the even more warming sight of Xavier's muscled legs and ass as he rummaged around in what looked like a gym bag on the floor.

He came back with a gift-wrapped package, a little larger and thicker than a ledger pad. Sitting back on his heels, he set it on the mattress where his body had left a shallow impression.

Doran was mystified. "What is it?"

Xavier winked at him. "A bribe."

"A bribe?" What in the world would he need a bribe for? There wasn't anything Doran wouldn't do for him without a second thought.

For a moment Xavier just looked at him, his brows drawn together over an unspoken question in his eyes, then he took a deep breath. "My parents have invited us to dinner tomorrow."

"No." It was out before Doran could think. Not this, not the scrutiny, the judgment, the inevitable dismissal. He couldn't.

There was a pause before Xavier said softly, "Okay."

Shit. "No" had been a shitty answer. *Wait. What?* "What do you mean, 'okay'?"

"Just okay. We don't have to go. Don't worry about it."

Come on, Callaghan. Xavier was giving him everything he'd ever dreamed of, and all he could come up with was "No"? "I mean, I can't . . . It's not that I . . . Oh god, I'm sorry, Xavier, I just don't think I can do this."

"Shhh, it's no big deal."

"Yes, it is, or you wouldn't have brought it up. It's important to you."

"Eventually." Xavier slipped back under the covers, the gift like a ticking bomb between them. "I don't have a lot of deep connections so, yeah, my parents are important to me. But it doesn't have to be now. They'll wait. It's nothing they wouldn't understand." He traced a finger along Doran's brow, smoothing out the crease Doran was never aware of making there. "They're good people. They're not going to kick you out or anything like that."

It was a little spooky how well Xavier read him. But comforting too. Nothing to hide. No stress. "What are they like?"

For a moment Xavier stared silently over Doran's shoulder. "When I got my first X-Men comic as a kid, I'd never heard the word adamantium before, but I already knew what it was. It was the stuff my mother was made of." He looked at Doran and smiled. "It was quite a shock to grow up and realize she was not indestructible." His gaze grew distant again. "It might have come as a shock to her too."

"What happened?"

"She had a stroke a couple of years ago. It affects her speech and one side of her body." He smiled, but there was some sadness in it. "Whatever you do, don't offer to help her with anything. She hates to be taken care of. I think it reminds her that there are things she can't do. She tends to forget otherwise."

He cupped Doran's face, and Doran felt his thumb along his upper lip. Then Xavier leaned in for a slow kiss, his hand under Doran's chin, his tongue and lips licking, tasting, sending little zings and sparkles through Doran's body.

"You're very distracting, you know that?" Xavier said, leaning back. "I keep forgetting what I'm talking about."

He was being distracting? What about Xavier making him feel like a million dollars? How was that not distracting?

"My father is easily the more nurturing of my parents," Xavier went on with a smile that said he knew exactly how solidly he'd derailed Doran's thoughts, and that he enjoyed it. "I think you'd like each other. You both have that artist's appreciation of beauty."

Doran chewed on his lip. Xavier wouldn't ask him to come if he didn't think he'd be okay. He ran a hand across the wrapping paper of the box. It didn't really matter what was inside; he owed Xavier a yes.

Not because it had been a command. It hadn't been. But because here, finally, was something he could do for Xavier.

Taking a deep breath, he slipped off the bow and ripped the paper. Then he stared at the wooden box in his hands, trying to sort through the wild roller-coaster ride of emotions it sent him on.

Xavier had bought him pencils. *The* pencils. The box of one flipping hundred art pencils and accessories that had haunted Doran's dreams for the past months. He wanted to say something. *Thank you*, for one, but nothing came out. And when he looked up, he got lost in the expression on Xavier's face. The one that said *I love you*, and *I'm going to spoil you rotten*.

"Can I try them?" he finally got out.

"Go wild," Xavier said. "They're yours. And just for the record, they were yours in any case."

Doran shook his head. "I'm okay with the dinner. I just, I panicked. It's stupid." He'd started to scramble out of bed with the box in his hand, but stopped himself. "I'd already decided I wanted to go before I opened it." He didn't want Xavier to think he was just going for the pencils. But then, Xavier had only called it a bribe so Doran wouldn't freak out about the expensive gift. Which it was. But, oh my god, it felt so good to run his hands across the surface of the pencils. He set the box on the table and dove for the pad in his backpack. He knew exactly what he wanted to draw.

Sunday morning started every bit as awesome as Saturday had ended. Though it was less edgy play, and more just deliciously slow lovemaking that left Doran a puddle on cloud nine when the sun was barely up.

But Sunday evening came fast enough to make anyone nervous. Xavier picked him up at the office just after five in faded jeans and a gray woolen sweater that had seen better days. Doran actually did a double take because even though Xavier dressed for comfort when he wasn't wearing the uniform, his clothes were usually neat and fairly new. At least Doran wouldn't stick out like a sore thumb. Which might have been his intention, unless dressing down was a thing at his parents' house.

He felt less nervous now with Xavier right next to him than he had at the office once his morning buzz had worn off, but he must still have fidgeted in his seat, because Xavier threw him a half-amused, half-understanding look and said, "You'll be fine. They'll love you. And not only because I do."

Easy to say. Some people didn't know what parents were capable of. What if they—

Wait. What? Doran stared at Xavier's profile, saw his Adam's apple move as he swallowed, registered the death grip on the steering wheel. But then Xavier blew out a puff of air and relaxed. He very briefly closed his eyes, no more than a long blink, and gave Doran a smile. "I do, you know? I love you."

Doran had to hold on to his seat hard to keep the happy racket that was exploding inside him from spilling straight into Xavier's lap. Why did he have to say that in the truck? While driving?

"I love you," he whispered, trying it out for himself, every muscle in his body tight with giddy energy. He looked at Xavier, who seemed to be having difficulties dividing his attention between Doran and the road. "I love you," Doran said louder.

A smile spread on Xavier's face, and when he looked at Doran again, his eyes mirrored what he'd just said and more. Like they had last night.

Doran gave up trying to contain his joy. He leaned back in his seat and started laughing. "I love you!" he yelled as loud as he could.

Xavier's smile grew into a wide grin. He pulled off the road into a long driveway. They must be almost at the south end of Bluewater Bay. A two-story log house came into view with a porch that wrapped around to the right, and a large garage on the left. The driveway looped in front of the house, with one lane forking off to a largish outbuilding on the left. Between that and the garage Doran could see the ground sloping gently down toward the West Twin River.

"Wow," he said, suddenly sober again. "This is where you grew up?"

Xavier nodded. "My father built everything you see." He pointed at the outbuilding. "The woodshed being built is one of my earliest memories. We added the garage the summer I turned twelve, when my father decided he wanted to try his own business. Don't ask me why everyone calls it the garage. It's his workshop."

As if conjured by his words, a giant of a man with a shock of gray-blond hair came out of the garage, wiping his hands on a rag. Xavier's height, but wider in the shoulders, with arms like small trees. He seemed deathly pale, but when he came closer Doran saw that he was just covered in sawdust.

Xavier climbed out and waved for Doran to follow him. "Papa, meet Doran Callaghan." And to Doran, "Karl Wagner, my father."

Doran expected his fingers to be crushed when they shook hands, but the big man's grip was merely firm, not punishing. "Thank you for the invitation, Mr. Wagner," Doran said.

Wagner smiled and pointed at Xavier. "Anyone who can put that kind of a smile on my son's face can call me Karl," he said.

Doran nodded, though he wasn't sure he'd be able to. He couldn't have been nicer, but there was something about Karl Wagner that commanded respect. Xavier had sure come by it honestly. Doran looked from one to the other, searching for similarities. Maybe in the smile, the height, but that was pretty much it.

Xavier's father herded them all into the house and excused himself to wash his hands.

"We're here, Ma," Xavier hollered up the stairs, but turned when his mother came out of the kitchen. She moved like a ship in heavy seas, using momentum to bring her right leg forward, then shifting her weight to a cane to take an almost normal step with her left. It looked awkward and labored, but when she stopped, she stood tall. Nearly as tall as Xavier. A lithe runner's body, still strong, despite the paralysis on the right side. Unable to shake hands with her one good hand holding the cane, she nodded a greeting, a regal gesture that fit her perfectly. She was beautiful. Xavier definitely got his looks from her. Doran's color brain picked a deep umber from the palette in his mind, with burnt sienna accents for the high cheekbones. She must have been absolutely stunning before her stroke.

He suddenly realized that Xavier had said something—introductions?—and he mumbled a mix of *thanks* and *honored*s that died a terrible death in embarrassment.

Dinner was scalloped potatoes and a green salad. Xavier and his dad ate about fifteen portions each and kept the conversation alive.

Doran managed to give reasonably sensible answers when asked a direct question and tried not to get caught staring at Xavier's mom. He wanted to draw her so bad that his fingers itched.

"So," Wagner said, "are you still contradicting yourself?"

Xavier shook his head. "No, I'm good. Better than good."

"That's what I thought." Wagner looked at Doran as if he was trying to figure something out. "Seems my lone wolf of a son discovered the comfort of well-matched companionship," he said slowly.

Xavier turned to Doran as well, but his eyes held that unholy light that flushed Doran with heat from his toes to his hairline. "Indeed."

Doran tried hard not to fidget in his chair. He was as turned on as he was embarrassed about it, until he realized that they were teasing him because that was what they did with each other, and he was part of that. Part of a real, normal family. Sunday dinners and all.

After dinner the men cleared the table, then piled into the kitchen for the dishes. And Doran loved every minute of it. He felt like he'd been adopted.

"Your parents are amazing," he said to Xavier later in the truck.

"Yup. They're pretty great as far as parents go," Xavier said with a fond smile.

Doran leaned his head against the backrest and watched the stars come out. He was grinning like a loon and couldn't stop. A line of an old Kenny Rogers song ran through his head. The one about gamblers knowing what to throw away or keep.

He must've been singing it under his breath because Xavier looked at him with one eyebrow drawn up. "Are you quoting country at me, boy?"

Doran's grin stayed on. "I have it coming, right?"

Instead of an answer, Xavier pulled over to reach for something in the backseat. He turned to Doran and handed him a coil of soft rope. "Hold that for me, would you?"

And just like that, those happy, sparkly bubbles exploded under his skin again. Exciting and carefree at the same time. Hell yeah, he'd hold that. All of it. As hard as he possibly could.

Explore more of *Bluewater Bay*:
riptidepublishing.com/titles/universe/bluewater-bay

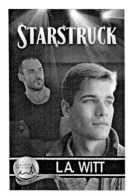

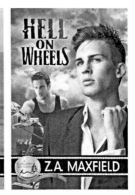

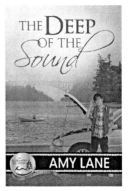

Dear Reader,

Thank you for reading G.B. Gordon's *When to Hold Them*!

We know your time is precious and you have many, many entertainment options, so it means a lot that you've chosen to spend your time reading. We really hope you enjoyed it.

We'd be honored if you'd consider posting a review—good or bad—on sites like **Amazon, Barnes & Noble, Kobo, Goodreads, Twitter, Facebook, Tumblr,** and your blog or website. We'd also be honored if you told your friends and family about this book. Word of mouth is a book's lifeblood!

For more information on upcoming releases, author interviews, blog tours, contests, giveaways, and more, please sign up for our weekly, spam-free newsletter and visit us around the web:

Newsletter: tinyurl.com/RiptideSignup
Twitter: twitter.com/RiptideBooks
Facebook: facebook.com/RiptidePublishing
Goodreads: tinyurl.com/RiptideOnGoodreads
Tumblr: riptidepublishing.tumblr.com

Thank you so much for Reading the Rainbow!

RiptidePublishing.com

ACKNOWLEDGMENTS

Many thanks, Chris, for being kind to a stranger and answering all my questions regarding park rangers so very patiently. Any mistakes are definitely mine.

Thank you, Marg, beta-reader extraordinaire, for never leaving me hanging.

And to Lori and Aleks for inviting me into the sandbox. I've enjoyed this immensely.

ALSO BY G. B. GORDON

Santuario
The Other Side of Winter

G.B. Gordon worked as a packer, landscaper, waiter, and coach before going back to school to major in linguistics and, at 35, switch to less backbreaking monetary pursuits like translating, editing, and writing.

Having lived in various parts of the world, Gordon is now happily ensconced in suburban Ontario with the best of all husbands.

Website and blog: gordon.kontext.ca
Twitter: twitter.com/gb_gordon
Goodreads: goodreads.com/gbgordon
Facebook: facebook.com/gb.gordon.5

Enjoy more stories like *When to Hold Them* at RiptidePublishing.com!

Blue Eyed Stranger
ISBN: 978-1-62649-213-4

Illumination
ISBN: 978-1-62649-051-2

Earn Bonus Bucks!

Earn 1 Bonus Buck for each dollar you spend. Find out how at RiptidePublishing.com/news/bonus-bucks.

Win Free Ebooks for a Year!

Pre-order coming soon titles directly through our site and you'll receive one entry into a drawing to win free books for a year! Get the details at RiptidePublishing.com/contests.

Lightning Source UK Ltd.
Milton Keynes UK
UKOW04f1954200715

255519UK00004B/249/P